Airball /

Airball /

MY LIFE IN BRIEFS

L. D. Harkrader

A DEBORAH BRODIE BOOK
ROARING BROOK PRESS
NEW MILFORD, CONNECTICUT

A Deborah Brodie Book

Published by Roaring Brook Press

Roaring Brook Press is a division of

Holtzbrinck Publishing Holdings Limited Partnership

143 West Street, New Milford, Connecticut 06776

Distributed in Canada by H. B. Fenn and Company, Ltd.

Library of Congress Cataloging-in-Publication Data

Harkrader, Lisa.

Airball : my life in briefs / L.D. Harkrader.

p. cm.

"A Deborah Brodie book."

Summary: Uncoordinated Kansas seventh-grader Kirby Nickel braves his
coach's ire and becomes captain of the basketball team in order to help him
prove that NBA star Brett McGrew is the father he has never known.

ISBN-13 978-1-59643-060-0

ISBN-10 1-59643-060-5

[1. Basketball—Fiction. 2. Fathers—Fiction. 3. Coaches
(Athletics)—Fiction. 4. Coaching (Athletics)—Fiction. 5. Kansas—Fiction.]

I. Title.

PZ7.H22615Air 2005

[Fic]—dc22

200403061

Roaring Brook Press books are available for special promotions and premiums.
For details, contact: Director of Special Markets, Holtzbrinck Publishers.

Book design by Jennifer Browne

Printed in the United States of America

First edition September 2005

2   4   6   8   10   9   7   5   3   1

For my parents,
who taught me that I could do anything.
L. D. H.

One

I should've suspected something.

The other guys whooped and dribbled around me, slapping balls out of each other's hands and charging in for layups at both ends of the court. Layups that mostly bounced wide of the basket.

For somebody like me, growing up in a basketball-loving family in a basketball-crazed town, you'd think I'd be screeching around the gym, too. You'd think I'd be rebounding every shot and sinking three-pointers from the lobby.

You'd think.

I just stood there on the free-throw line, in the shadow of that big orange sign above the scoreboard, clutching a basketball tight to my chest. Outside, a wild October wind whipped through town, rattling the windows high above the bleachers in the gym. The very air felt like change. Like anything could happen.

You know the kid who kicks the ball out of bounds when he dribbles? The kid whose jump shots look like bounce passes? The kid who spends most of the game skidding across the floor on his face? That's me. Last summer my own grandmother beat me in a game of H-O-R-S-E.

I studied that orange sign and tried to imagine what it

1

felt like to be six-foot-nine with a gym full of fans cheering and chanting my name. *Kirby. Kir-by. KIR-BY!*

"Hey, Kirby, if you're just going to stand there like a jockstrap, give us the ball."

Russell Wiles and Eddie Poggemeyer thundered past.

"And get out of the way."

I pried the basketball from my chest and thumped it on the floor. I eyed the basket and thumped again. I lined up the ball, flexed my knees, and shot, flicking my wrist like Brett McGrew.

The ball hit the rim and bounced straight back. About knocked me over.

My cousin Bragger chased it into the bleachers.

"Your aim's good," he said, "but you need a little more arc." He curled one hand up over his head, then down, demonstrating arc. "You get that, Kirby, you'll be a starter."

"Right."

"Seriously."

"They have this rule, Bragger. To be a starter, you actually have to be on the team. And I'm not going out for basketball, remember?"

"That's what you keep saying." He twirled the ball in his hands. "Who holds the NBA record for most points in a single game?"

"You already know."

"I forgot."

I rolled my eyes. "Wilt Chamberlain. One hundred points against the Knicks. March 2, 1962."

"How many rebounds did Brett McGrew pull down in the NCAA championship game his senior year?"

"Twenty-four," I said. "Why?"

He shrugged. "You love basketball, Kirby."

"I can't *play* basketball, Bragger. And I don't need an after-school athletics program to prove it."

He shrugged again. "Can't be a hero if you're afraid of looking stupid."

"No problem then, because I don't want to be a hero."

"Sure you do, Kirby. Everybody does. Down deep inside, everybody wants to be a hero."

"Not me."

Bragger twirled the ball again. "Guess it's up to me to lead the team to victory."

He dribbled in place, charged the basket, and shot. Airball. Bragger didn't care. He ran after it, snagged it as it rolled into the wrestling mats, and lobbed it up over the backboard to me.

I let it bounce right past. Because that's when I heard the growl. Deep, low, and gurgling, like a water heater about to blow. I knew that growl. It was Coach Armstrong. Coach "Iron Man" Mike Armstrong. Our new gym teacher. Favorite saying: "Practice till you puke." Favorite aroma: sweat. Favorite hobby: watching me run extra laps because I couldn't climb a rope, steal a base, or sink a free throw.

That's all I'd learned about him since he took over the seventh grade P.E. program at the beginning of the school year. But that's all I needed to know.

Well, that and one other thing: When Coach growls, it means he's about to yell at somebody. Usually whoever's moving the slowest. Usually Kirby Nickel.

Me.

He marched over and stopped in front of me, his nostrils puffed out so wide I could see his nose hairs quivering inside. His whistle was clenched between his teeth, and from the way his cheek muscles were knotted up, I thought for sure that whistle would snap in two.

But he wasn't looking at me. He was glaring at the bleachers, his stubby blond flattop standing at attention above his raging red face. "Nickel!" He spit my name out around the whistle. "How long have *they* been here?"

I swiveled sideways.

And that's when I should've suspected something. Mrs. Zimmer, the school board president, was seated in the first row of bleachers. She sat there straight as a thorn, a big black notebook open on her lap. Every time one of the guys took a shot, Mrs. Zimmer scribbled something in the book. Every time they missed, she pressed her lips into a grim line and wrote something else.

Mr. Dobbs, the vice president, sat beside her. He wasn't scribbling in a notebook, and he didn't seem interested in the players. He was leaning back, elbows propped on the bench behind him, John Deere hat pushed back on his head, staring at the big orange sign over the scoreboard. The one that said:

4

Welcome to Stuckey
The Basketball Capital of Kansas
Home of the Great Brett McGrew

Coach clenched and unclenched his fists, then blew his whistle. Right in my ear.

The guys stopped screeching around the gym and gathered at the free-throw line. I sidled up alongside them. Coach whirled to face us. A stack of papers fluttered against his clipboard. Institutional green, neatly stapled at the corners.

"Permission slips," Bragger whispered.

"You people think you can play basketball?" Coach thumped a finger against the papers. "If so, you need one of these."

He started passing the papers out. The other guys crowded in around him. I stood off to one side. No sense getting in anybody's way.

Coach handed a permission slip to Eddie Poggemeyer. "First page is for your parents."

Sure, I'd come watch. Like Bragger said, I love basketball. From the bleachers.

"Second page"—Coach slapped permission slips into the outstretched hands of Russell Wiles and Duncan Webber—"is the physical form."

I might even keep unofficial stats on the players. I couldn't pass, shoot, or dribble, but I could figure percentages in a coma. Being a basketball fan and a citizen of the

Basketball Capital of Kansas, I owed it to my fellow seventh graders to support the team.

"You want to play basketball, get both pages signed."

But I didn't need to put on a uniform and invite the entire town down to the gym to watch me look pathetic. No way.

"This year we have an added bonus."

No way. No how.

Coach pushed a permission slip toward me. "Brett McGrew."

Two

I blinked. "Brett McGrew?"

"Are you deaf, Nickel? Yeah, Brett McGrew." Coach was still dangling the permission slip in front of me. He narrowed his eyes and studied me for a long moment. "You going to take this or not?"

I peeled one arm loose from my chest and snatched it from his hand. I scanned the page for Brett McGrew's name.

Coach circled back to the front of the class. "The University of Kansas is retiring Brett McGrew's jersey at a KU game in Lawrence this coming February. Big, momentous occasion." Coach puffed out his nostrils. "National press coverage, big-name guests, everybody getting teary-eyed. To make the whole thing even more special, the university has invited Stuckey to send a basketball team to represent Brett McGrew's hometown. Our school board, in their infinite wisdom"—Coach glanced at the bleachers—"chose us."

"Us?" Eddie Poggemeyer narrowed his eyes. "You mean, like, the seventh-grade team?"

"Yeah," said Coach. "I mean, like, the seventh-grade team. You got a problem with that?"

"No, but why—"

"Because if you've got a problem, I can talk to the school board, see if they'll send—"

"No!"

"Didn't think so." Coach tucked his clipboard under his arm. "So. You sign up for basketball, you play your little buns off, you get to meet the big hero. First practice is a week from Monday. Be here. On time. When Brett McGrew meets this team, I want him to see he's not the only basketball player that ever came from this town." He blew his whistle again. "Line up, gentlemen. It's not every day we have esteemed members of our school board" —he said "school board" like he had gristle caught in his teeth—"right here in our gym. Let's show 'em what we're made of."

I already knew what we were made of, and I would've voted that we keep it to ourselves. But Coach wasn't taking suggestions. He herded us together for a layup drill.

I folded the permission slip, tucked it into my sock, and meandered back toward my usual place at the end of the line.

Bragger grabbed my arm. "Here's your chance, Kirb."

I looked at him. "Chance for what?"

"Chance to get Coach on your side."

"My side? Why?"

Bragger didn't answer. He elbowed his way toward the front of the line, dragging me along behind. He shoved me ahead of him and stood there grinning like a jack-o'-lantern.

I knew that grin. It was a bad sign. It was the same grin

he flashed at the school nurse just before he volunteered me to read the captions on the *Welcome to Puberty* slide show.

Bragger says he got his nickname because when he was little, he couldn't pronounce his real name, Brandon. He says it always came out "Bragger," and everybody thought it was so cute, they started calling him that, too.

Grandma says that part's true enough, but the name wouldn't have stuck if it didn't fit so well. Which wouldn't be so bad if he'd just stick to bragging about himself. But he always has to brag other people into his mess of trouble, too.

People who frequently turn out to be me.

Coach clapped his hands. "Let's show a little hustle." He swung around and saw me standing at the front of the line. He stopped mid-clap. "You going first, Nickel?"

I swallowed. "Well, no, I just—"

"Sure he is, Coach," said Bragger. "He's got a great shot—Brett McGrew's famous spinning layup."

"*Brag*-ger." I glared at him.

Coach chewed on his whistle. "Spinning layup, huh?" He glanced at Mrs. Zimmer, then turned back to me and narrowed his eyes. "Think you can pull it off?"

"Well, no, I—"

"Sure he can, Coach." Bragger grinned at him, then leaned toward me. "It'll be okay, Kirby," he whispered. "You've been practicing this layup since you were born."

"But I never got it right."

"Exactly. But now your butt's on the line. You *got* to

make this shot. You'll have all that adrenaline pumping through your veins." He kneaded my shoulders. "Trust the adrenaline, Kirby."

Coach blew his whistle. "You two can do therapy on your own time," he snarled. "I want to see this spinning layup." He leaned forward till his nose practically touched mine. His hot breath whiffed out onto my upper lip. "And don't embarrass me." He shoved a basketball into my gut.

I nodded and swallowed.

Coach licked his teeth. The other players crowded around. Mrs. Zimmer watched, her pen poised over her notebook.

"Dribble, Kirby," Bragger whispered.

Dribble. *Right.*

I thumped the ball in front of me and started running. At least, I think I was running. I could see one foot, then the other, shoot out in front of me. I could see the lines on the floor disappear behind me. I could hear the ball bouncing—*thonk, thonk, thonk*—perilously close to the toe of my right sneaker as my shoes *thwap*ped against the wood.

Thonk.

Thwap.

Thonk.

Thwap.

With each step I knew I'd kick it. Kick it out of bounds and into the bleachers.

But I didn't. I kept dribbling. Dribbling and dribbling and dribbling, for miles it seemed, until I couldn't feel my arm, couldn't feel my hand pumping up and down, couldn't feel the nubby roughness of the ball.

"Shoot, Kirby!"

Shoot. *Right.*

I pulled the ball up, took my final step, and leaped.

"There he goes." Bragger's voice echoed through the rafters. "Brett McGrew's famous spinning layup."

I spun, all right. Up and around and around again. I kept on spinning till my legs and feet were practically braided together. Then gravity kicked in, and down I came.

Splat.

Belly first. The ball looped out of bounds. I lay on the cold, polished wood, breathing shoe grit and floor wax.

Coach blew his whistle.

I peeled my cheek off the floor. I could see Mrs. Zimmer scribbling in her black book.

Mr. Dobbs shook his head. He unfolded himself from his seat and ambled across the gym toward the lobby.

"I'm not sure Brett McGrew himself could help this bunch," he muttered as the door clanked shut behind him.

Three

Folks around here claim Brett McGrew could dribble before he could walk and could make a jump shot by the time he reached kindergarten. They say he got the nickname "Brett McNet" when he sank fifty-seven three-pointers in a row one morning during ninth-grade P.E. They say he grew to be six feet tall drinking warm milk straight from the cows on his daddy's dairy farm, then grew another nine inches doing pull-ups on the hay hook in the barn.

I don't know if all that's true. But I do know Brett McGrew never got the wind knocked out of him running in for an uncontested layup.

"You didn't look half bad going up," Bragger said. "Gotta work on that dismount, though."

We shuffled through a little whirlpool of brown leaves on the sidewalk. School had just let out, and Bragger and I were headed over to the Double Dribble Cafe for a Coke. I still had the permission slip tucked in my sock. The neatly stapled corner was rubbing a sore spot on my ankle.

I should've pulled it out right then. Pulled it out and let it blow away in the wind. Blow away with the leaves and the dust, down the street, past the grain elevator, and out of my life.

That would've been the smart thing.

Of course, that would've been littering, too, which, according to Grandma, is a sign of weak character, right up there with lying, cussing, and goaltending.

We reached the Double Dribble. Bragger swung the door open. The little bell jangled against the glass, and the aroma of warm onions and dead french fries billowed out at us. A table of farmers, in for their afternoon coffee, glanced up, saw we weren't worth stopping their jawing and guffawing for, and went back to their discussion of Lloyd Metcalf's fancy new combine.

Mrs. Snodgrass saw us, too, and started filling two glasses with ice and Coke. Bragger headed straight for the counter.

I squatted down by the glass case under the cash register. Inside were trading cards and pencils and little pennants that said, "I ate at the Double Dribble Cafe in Stuckey, Kansas, home of Brett McGrew." The T-shirts said that, too. So did the menus, and if you wanted to keep your menu, Mrs. Snodgrass would sell it to you for three dollars.

There was only one thing Mrs. Snodgrass wouldn't sell, and I knew, because I'd asked so many times she wouldn't answer anymore. It was one particular menu lying in tissue paper in the center of the top shelf. It was yellowed and dog-eared and had a big ketchup stain down one side.

But that wasn't why she wouldn't sell it.

She wouldn't sell it because on the other side, right

over SIDE ORDERS, was Brett McGrew's big, scrawling autograph:

> To Mrs. Snodgrass, who makes the best
> biscuits and gravy on the planet.
> Brett "McNet" McGrew #5

The pen he wrote it with was lying in the tissue, too. Medium blue ballpoint. Brett McGrew's teeth marks on the cap.

I squinted at that menu, trying to find some resemblance between Brett McGrew's looping, confident signature and my own scratchy handwriting.

Mrs. Snodgrass thumped me on the head. "You're fogging up the glass again, Kirby." Her Brillo-pad voice rattled in her chest. "Go on and drink your Coke. You got better stuff than that at home."

She was right. I did. I had cards and mugs and posters and team schedules and a gym towel Eddie Poggemeyer swore his uncle caught during the last game of the Final Four when Brett McGrew flung it into the crowd after winning the NCAA Championship. Cost me sixteen bucks and a McNet Rookie Year NBA Frisbee, but it was worth it. It had Brett McGrew's dried sweat all over it.

I stood up and threaded my way through the tables to the counter. I slid onto the stool next to Bragger's. He'd already sucked his glass empty and was chewing on the ice.

"Grandma's going to faint when you tell her you're going out for basketball," he said. "She'll sign your permission slip first, of course. Then she'll pass out cold."

Yep. I could see it: Grandma, unconscious with joy.

I peeled the paper from one end of my straw. "Do me a favor, okay?" I blew on the straw. The paper shot off the end, flipped through the air, and landed in Bragger's glass. "Don't make a big deal out of it when we get to my house."

Bragger fished the paper out of his ice. "Why?"

Why? Because sometimes the things you want just aren't possible, that's why. Sometimes they're not even good for you. Sometimes thinking about what *might* be, what's potentially possible in some far-off future, is better than finding out the thing you want most in the world doesn't want you back.

But that's not what I told Bragger. What I told Bragger was, "No reason. It's just, you know, I'm not exactly basketball material, as my amazing belly flop this morning demonstrated."

Bragger shrugged. "Basketball players eat the floor all the time. On purpose, if they think they can get a charging foul called. You know what Coach says: 'You don't get floor burns, you're not playing hard enough.'" He gave me a sideways grin. "He's going to love you."

"Thanks." I flipped ice at him.

But my heart wasn't in it.

It was funny. I'd been keeping this same secret for nearly thirteen years. And for most of that time, it had seemed like an ordinary part of my life. Like something that occasionally wanted to burst out, but for the most part stayed right where it belonged: buried inside my gut.

15

But now, today, ever since Coach had uttered those two fateful words—"Brett McGrew"—the stress had been building to the point where I thought it was going to start popping through my skin. Like water shooting through rust holes in a pipe.

I sucked in a long sip of Coke. And swallowed. "There's something else," I said.

Bragger nodded. "I figured."

"There's also"—I took a deep breath—"my father."

Bragger looked at me. "Your *father*?"

His voice echoed through the Double Dribble, drowning out the country-and-western station blaring from the radio propped up on the Coke machine. The coffee drinkers stopped their jawing and guffawing. Mrs. Snodgrass came to a dead halt with one hand on the coffeepot and the other halfway in the pie case. They all stared at us for one petrifying moment, then shook their heads over the way kids these days act in public, and turned back to their own business.

I jabbed Bragger with my elbow. "Keep your voice down," I hissed. "I'd rather not have my family's personal business spread across three counties by supper time."

"Family business?" Bragger shook his head, obviously confused. But he did lower his voice. "What family business? I don't mean to be harsh, Kirb, but your family consists of you and Grandma. That's it. You don't have a father."

"Everyone has a father."

"Technically, yeah. But—and again, I don't mean to be

harsh—he died. Before you were born. You never even met him. Nobody did. Not even Grandma."

"Yes, she did."

"She did?" He leaned closer, his eyes wide. "She told you?"

"No. She didn't have to. I know she met him because my father"—I glanced around to see if Mrs. Snodgrass was listening, but she was still busy filling the pie case— "because my father"—I sneaked a look at the coffee drinkers, who were still in deep discussion over the power seat on Lloyd Metcalf's combine—"because my father"—I lowered my voice to barely a whisper—"is Brett McGrew."

There. I'd said it. It could stop popping through my skin.

"Brett McGrew?" Bragger blinked. Then nodded. "Good one, Kirb." He thumped me in the arm. "You had me going there."

"I'm not kidding."

He raised an eyebrow.

"Think about it," I said. "My middle name is Michael."

"So?"

"So Brett McGrew's middle name is Michael."

Bragger looked at me. "Duncan Webber's middle name is Michael. My dad's middle name is Michael. Heck, Coach's *first* name is Michael. Everybody's named Michael. And guess what? Brett McGrew is not their father."

"No," I said. "He's not. But he *is* mine." I sucked up the rest of my Coke and thumped the glass down on the counter. "And I can prove it."

Four

It was starting to get dark by the time we reached my yard, but the wind hadn't died down. It whistled through the tall elms that circled the big, old two-story house Grandma and I lived in and pelted Bragger and me with dust and leaves.

We clomped up the steps to the back porch. I swung the door open. The wind caught hold and about jerked it away from me. I held on with both hands as Bragger and I squeezed inside, then hauled it shut and latched it. The wind rattled against the glass like it wasn't finished with us yet. Like it was trying to beat its way inside to go another round.

We draped our jackets over the mound of old coats hanging on hooks beside the upright freezer, then tromped into the house.

Grandma was banging around, fixing supper. She tugged on the oven door. It screeched open, and a puff of smoke belched out. The smoke wrapped around her, the same color as her hair, so that for a second I couldn't see her head, only a cloud of smoke with skinny pants poking out the bottom.

Grandma waved the smoke away with a dish towel. Bragger and I headed straight for the back staircase.

"I'm home," I said as we barreled up the steps.

"Nice to see you, too," she hollered after us. "Don't get too involved in anything. Supper'll be ready soon."

"We won't," I hollered back.

Bragger and I bounded into my room and dumped our backpacks on my bottom bunk.

"Be quiet," I said. "And take your shoes off."

Bragger raised his eyebrows, but he didn't say anything.

We kicked our shoes under my bed and crept sock-footed across the big, square second-floor hall into my mother's old room. I eased the door shut behind us and waited till I heard the soft click of the latch before I flipped the light switch. Wicker furniture gleamed clean and white under the overhead light.

I stood there for a minute and took it in. My mother's hats hanging on the wooden rack above her antique iron bed. Her bulletin board bursting with music awards. Her cassette tapes lined up in a neat row beside a clunky old stereo that was invented before they invented CDs.

I ran my sock feet through the thick pink rug. With nobody actually living here, you'd think the room would be dusty and dim. But Grandma vacuumed and polished once a week. It was the only room she never made me help clean.

Bragger flopped onto the bed. The prehistoric metal bedsprings let out a screech.

"*Brag*-ger," I said.

"Sorry." He crept to the edge of the bed and managed

to sit up without setting off the bedsprings again.

"Okay." I took a big breath. "The first piece of evidence."

I pulled a red fake-leather book from the bookcase. It was her yearbook. My mother's senior yearbook.

I eased onto the edge of the bed next to Bragger and set the book on my lap. It naturally fell open to the senior pictures. My gaze naturally fell to the middle of the page, to the skinny girl with wild hair. Curly like mine, only hers was red instead of blond, and so long it flowed past her shoulders and right out of the picture.

I ran my finger over her name. *Melissa Nickel.* I slid my finger to the picture before hers, right beside her in alphabetical order: Brett McGrew. Over the corner, in his big, loopy handwriting, he'd scrawled, *To Missy. Love always, Brett.*

"Look what he wrote." I smoothed the yearbook out flat. "He said he'd love her always."

Bragger leaned over my arm so he could see. "No, he didn't. He said 'Love always.' That's what people say, Kirby. He probably wrote it in everybody's yearbook. He would've written it on Mrs. Snodgrass's menu if she'd asked him. You can't base your whole family tree on two words scribbled in a yearbook. That's no better than having your middle name be Michael."

"Not by itself, no. But there's more." I flipped through the pages. "I didn't just start this yesterday, you know. I've been working on it a while. Ever since I was old enough to figure out what a father is and that I'm the only kid around who doesn't have one. I've been gathering clues, one by one, and the evidence is overwhelming." I found the page I was looking for. "There. That's them." I set the book on Bragger's lap. "My mother and Brett McGrew. Dancing."

Bragger studied the picture. "Dorky clothes."

"And look at what it says." I pointed to the top of the page. "King and Queen of the Sweetheart Dance. The *Sweetheart* Dance."

"You weren't paying attention to the *Welcome to Puberty* slide show, were you, Kirb? You don't get born just because your mom danced with a basketball player. Look." He pointed to a picture on the next page. "Here she is again, dancing with some other guy. Can't see his face, but he's not tall enough to be Brett McGrew. And look how close they're dancing. She's not snuggled up that close to McNet."

"Probably a slow song," I said. "You're supposed to dance close to slow songs."

"Are you supposed to close your eyes? Cause hers are closed."

"Blinking," I said. "I imagine she blinked right when the photographer snapped the picture."

Bragger gave me a pitiful look. "Okay, Kirby, let's say you're right. There's not a chance in the universe Brett McGrew is your father, but let's feed your delusional fantasy for a minute and say he is. Why didn't your mother ever mention it? Why would she dump you on Grandma

21

here in Nowhere, Kansas, if you had a perfectly good father out in Phoenix, Arizona? If you could be lounging around his mansion, swimming in his pool, driving his Porsche, and getting free tickets to the play-offs? Why?"

"I wondered that very thing," I said. "Because it doesn't seem to make sense."

"Not a lick of sense, Kirby. Not a *lick* of *sense*."

"But here's my theory. Think what it must've been like back then, when Brett McGrew was in high school. He's fielding scholarship offers from all over the country. He's traveling to KU and Duke and Kentucky and who knows where else to check out college programs. He's going to be a big-time basketball star, and everybody knows it. Everybody in town's helping him get there the best way they can. Everybody. Including my mother. You really think she's going to saddle him with a baby? Hold him back from everything he always wanted?"

"Or here's another theory. Maybe she didn't saddle him with a baby because he's *not your father*." Bragger gave me a sympathetic poke in the ribs with his elbow. "Look, Kirby. It totally bites that you don't have a mom or a dad. But hallucinating about Brett McGrew isn't going to fix anything."

I didn't say anything. I slid the bottom drawer of my mother's dresser open and pulled out a flat, tissue-wrapped bundle. I folded the tissue back and held it up so Bragger could see. It was the clincher I'd saved for last: a red basketball jersey, neatly folded so the white satin letters that spelled out Stuckey were perfectly centered above a huge number 5.

"Whoa." Bragger touched the jersey. Gently. With the very tips of his fingers, as if the fabric might disintegrate beneath his hands if he pressed too hard. He leaned down and sniffed.

"Doesn't smell like sweat."

"No. It smells like old dresser drawer."

He pulled his nose from the fabric. "You been holding out on me, Kirbster. You didn't tell me you had a real live Brett McGrew jersey."

"I don't," I said. "My mother did. Know where I found it?"

Bragger shrugged. "In her dresser?"

"In the *bottom drawer* of her dresser."

Bragger wrinkled his forehead, obviously not getting it.

"The same drawer where she stored my baby footprints."

Forehead still wrinkled. Still not comprehending.

"Same drawer," I said, "where she stashed my coming-home-from-the-hospital clothes."

Bragger looked at me. Forehead still wrinkled. But he nodded.

"Same drawer," I said, "where she kept the flowers she wore to the Sweetheart Dance. The flowers she was wearing when she danced with Brett McGrew. The flowers she saved by pressing them between the pages of my baby book, which"—I unfolded the jersey and pulled out a satin-covered book with my squalling newborn picture on the front—"I found wrapped up inside."

Bragger's gaze flickered to the baby book, then back to me. "Same drawer?"

I nodded. "Same drawer."

He ran his fingers over the jersey again.

"Okay," he said. "I'm convinced. Number five is your father."

Five

"You don't really look like him." Bragger studied Brett McGrew's senior picture. We'd smuggled my mother's yearbook back across the hall to my room, and Bragger was lounging on his stomach on my bottom bunk with the yearbook spread open on the pillow.

"I know," I said. "I keep thinking there has to be a resemblance, but I can't find it."

"Maybe it's not so much in the face. Maybe it's in your build. Maybe you're built like McNet."

He flipped through the yearbook till he found an action shot of Brett McGrew muscling his way around a Whipple player to make a shot. Bragger swung around to a sitting position and held the yearbook on his lap. He looked back and forth from me to the picture.

"You didn't get his height," he said. "Not so far, anyway. Maybe you're a late bloomer."

"Maybe." I was sitting on the edge of the bed. My feet didn't even reach the floor. I'd hate to think I was an early bloomer and this was all I got.

"You're not as muscle-bound as he is. Look at his legs. Even in high school he was a human catapult." He glanced at my legs. At my bony, white, hairless legs, the kneecaps sticking up like tumors on a toothpick. "He probably worked out more than you do."

"I imagine so."

"But look here. Look at his shoulders, how wide they are." He held the yearbook up. "And look at yours."

I looked. He looked. At Brett McGrew's biceps bulging from the arms of his jersey. Then at my own scrawny shoulders. Barely wider than my ears. Bones practically poking through the skin.

"Maybe it's not a resemblance you can catch in a picture," said Bragger. "Maybe it's something you have to see in person. It'll be easy to see once you're standing there right next to him in Lawrence. Right next to Brett McGrew." He shook his head. "I still can't believe it. Brett McGrew. Your father."

"He doesn't know he's my father."

"Not yet. But he will. Hey, you're going to let me lounge by the pool with you, aren't you? And drive the Porsche? I mean, you know, once we're old enough to get a learner's permit."

I didn't say anything.

Bragger glanced up. "Oh, man." He shook his head. "I know that look. The look that means you're thinking too hard. You *are* going to tell him, right? You're going out for basketball, you're meeting Brett McGrew, and you're telling him he's your father. I mean, that's the whole point."

"You'd think."

"You'd think? What do you mean, 'you'd think'? This is your big chance, Kirby. If you don't take it, you might not ever get another one."

"I know."

"I mean, he's a major sports figure. You can't just walk up to him on the street. He's probably got bodyguards."

"I know."

"And you can't call him, like he was a regular person or something. His number's probably unlisted. You could write him a letter, but it'd probably go right to the Brett McGrew Fan Club or the Suns front office or something. He'd never even see it. And I doubt you could get his e-mail address. Not his real one, anyway."

"I know. You think I haven't thought about all this?"

"So this is it, Kirby. This is your chance. It's, like, your destiny or something."

Huh. My destiny. Courtesy of Mrs. Zimmer. And Coach.

"You can't fight destiny," said Bragger. "You go to Lawrence, you meet your father, you complete your destiny. That's how it works."

"No, that's not how it works. I've thought about this, and I can't see how it *could* work. What am I supposed to say? 'Glad to meet you, Mr. McGrew. Thanks for inviting us. By the way, turns out we've got a lot in common—our DNA.' That'd go over real well right there in the middle of the fieldhouse, with TV cameras and sports writers lurking around. Not to mention Coach. He'd wad me into a ball and drop-kick me to Nebraska. And that's not even the worst part."

Bragger looked at me. "There's worse? Worse than Coach?"

"Yeah. Worse than Coach." I grabbed the yearbook from him and held Brett McGrew's picture up next to me. "If you were this guy"—I pointed to McNet —"would you want anything to do with this guy?" I flung my hand up beside my own scrawny self. "Would you even admit you were related?"

Bragger shrugged. "You're related to me and I admit it."

"Not the same thing."

"I don't know what you're getting all worked up about, Kirby. So you don't look like your father. So what?"

"It's not just the way I look. It's the way I *am*. Brett McGrew has been the MVP of every team he's ever played for. Me, I shoot a layup and practically end up in the nurse's office. I'm not what he wants in a son."

Bragger considered this. "You're right," he said. "Brett McGrew probably has very specific taste in offspring. I imagine he'd want somebody more like your mother was. You know—tall and muscular, talented in every sport, leading her team to victory with her unequaled skill and athleticism."

"What are you talking about?" I looked at him. "My mother was short and skinny and, as far as I know, never went out for a sport in her life. I found her report cards. She flunked P.E."

Bragger shook his head. "Weird."

"What?"

"You just described yourself."

"I *know*. That's the problem. Have you not been listening?"

28

Bragger took the yearbook from me and flipped through it till he found the Sweetheart Dance page. He set the book in my lap.

"Your mother was just like you, Kirby. And guess what? McNet liked her anyway."

I stared at the picture. The same picture I'd been staring at my whole life. But I'd never truly looked at it before. Not really. My mother *had* been just like me. Same freckles. Same bony shoulders sticking out of her glittery Sweetheart Dance dress. She was short, too. Even in high heels, she barely came up to Brett McGrew's armpit.

I looked closer. "I think she's stepping on his foot."

Bragger leaned over my shoulder. "Hey, she is. Her spiky heel's totally skewering Brett McGrew's big toe." He shrugged. "McNet doesn't seem to mind."

No, he didn't. Brett McGrew was smiling down at her, and she had her neck bent back, laughing up at him. My short, skinny, clumsy mother. Brett McGrew liked her.

Brett McGrew liked her.

"What we need is a plan," said Bragger.

Brett McGrew liked her.

"Are you with me, Kirb? A plan. To get you through all the reporters and TV cameras. And past Coach. A plan to get you into a private conversation with Brett McGrew."

I looked up. "How are we supposed to do that?"

"We'll think of something. We've got a lot going for us here. You're the smartest kid in Stuckey, and I"—he stopped, obviously considering his talents—"I am the most willing to make a complete fool of myself. That's

29

a powerful combination, Kirby. Together, nobody can stop us."

I stared at him. He was right. If I was going to do this, I had to plan out every detail. And I could do that. Better than anybody. This could work. It could.

Six

Grandma called us for supper. Bragger always ate with us on days his parents worked late. I slid my mother's yearbook under my pillow, and Bragger and I sock-footed it downstairs in time to see Grandma slide a big pan from the oven.

It was her turkey roaster. But the steaming mound of meat inside it was like no turkey I'd ever seen. It was huge and round and coated with something gleaming and blackened in spots, like ketchup, only orange, with darker stripes running across it in a vaguely familiar pattern.

It was a meatloaf, I realized. An enormous meatloaf.

In the shape of a basketball.

"Whoa," said Bragger.

"What do you think?" said Grandma.

"It's, it's . . . wow," I said.

Which was my standard mealtime response. My grandmother has many talents. Cooking isn't one of them. Nobody ever mentions this to her, of course. No sense hurting her feelings, especially after she's gone to so much trouble. She wouldn't believe it anyway. Criticism just leads to more creativity on her part, in an attempt to prove everybody wrong, and, as Bragger's dad says, if she gets too much more creative, we'll need our stomachs pumped.

But she'd obviously been cooking all afternoon, and now she stood clutching her masterpiece, her eyes shining with pride behind her steamed-over glasses.

"Seriously, Grandma," I said. "It's the best meatloaf I've ever seen."

Grandma nodded, her proud, shiny gaze landing on me. She made her way across the kitchen, the turkey roaster balanced carefully between her oven mitts. My grandmother isn't very big, maybe an inch taller than I am, and that meatloaf had a good ten pounds on her.

"Need some help?" I said.

"Nope. I got it. You two just find your places."

She lowered the roaster onto the ancient chrome-legged kitchen table, in the spot she'd saved for it next to the gravy. She stood back and took a minute to admire her work. I knew she'd never reveal the secret of the orange ketchup coating, but I suspect she'd thrown some mustard into the mix.

What Grandma's meals lack in flavor and chewability, they make up for in sheer volume. I could barely see the Formica tabletop under all the bowls and platters she'd set out: lumpy mashed potatoes, lumpier gravy, a plate of sliced tomatoes, her crystal pickle dish full of limp home-canned pickles, her usual three-bean salad freshened up with a new ingredient that looked suspiciously like okra, carrot Jell-O that hadn't quite set up and was sloshing around in a recycled butter tub.

And the fifty-pound meatloaf.

Bragger and I took our usual places, while Grandma rummaged around in the junk drawer next to the sink. She pulled out a pen and shoved the drawer shut with her hip.

"So," she said, "I didn't fix this big dinner for nothing. Are you going to give me that permission slip so I can sign it?"

I took a deep breath, looked at Bragger, and nodded. I dug the green stapled paper out of my sock, and handed it to her. She held it at arm's length and peered at it through her bifocals, obviously eager to sign me up for a season of humiliation.

She flipped to the second page and scanned the physical form. "I made an appointment for you with Doc Houston in the morning, so you'll be all set."

She flipped back to the front page and clicked her pen. She scratched her even, no-frills signature across the bottom of the permission slip, clicked the pen again, and nodded.

And just like that, I was off to meet my destiny.

Seven

The lunch lady heaped a mound of toxic waste onto my tray and slid it across the cafeteria window. I clanked my fork and spoon into their slot, picked up the tray, and followed Bragger across the clatter and noise of the lunchroom.

He stopped when he reached The Hulk. The metal was rusted, the plasticized top was chipping off, and one leg was bent so crooked the lunch ladies had to stuff a wad of napkins under it to keep the whole thing from toppling over. It was the most beat-up table in the cafeteria, shoved into the far corner under a light fixture that buzzed and flickered, an obvious threat to public safety. Nobody ever sat there unless they were unlucky enough to get to the lunchroom after all the other tables were filled up.

Today, as usual, The Hulk was empty. Perfect. Bragger and I needed to talk strategy, and we couldn't risk anybody hearing us. Over the weekend, we'd developed a basic plan to get me into a private conversation with Brett McGrew. Now we needed to finalize the details.

We glanced around to see who was within earshot. Eddie Poggemeyer and Russell Wiles were at the next table over, but they had their backs to us, plus they were too busy shooting peas out of their nostrils to notice what Bragger and I were doing.

We slid our trays onto the table and scooted into our chairs. I dropped my backpack to the floor.

Step One of The Plan was to make the basketball team. In Stuckey, population 334, this would be one of the easier accomplishments of my life. We had only twelve boys in the whole seventh grade, so as long as I showed up to practice, I would not only make the team, I might, as Bragger pointed out, see some playing time.

I'd have to guard against that.

Step Two: Make Brett McGrew sit up and take notice. Since I'd probably get only a second or two of McNet's time at the KU game, maybe long enough to shake his hand and say, "I'm really honored to—" before I got herded out of the way so McNet could shake hands with the next kid, I needed to find something, some piece of evidence, that would grab his attention in an instant. That would make him curious enough to at least listen to me.

"I've been thinking about this." I poked my fork into the heap of toxic waste. Goulash, according to the lunch menu, but I'd never seen goulash with such a green tinge before, not even Grandma's on one of her more creative days. "The best evidence would be something visual. Something I could just hold up, sort of flash at him, no talking or explaining involved."

"Right. Since talking and explaining isn't your strong suit." Bragger spooned a glob of goulash into his mouth— he liked to live dangerously—and chewed thoughtfully for a moment. "The best thing to flash would be a picture of him that looks like you, at least a little bit. I mean, everybody says I look like my dad, right? But everybody also says I have my mom's smile. So we just need to find that one little part of Brett McGrew that looks like you."

I rolled a pea around my tray as I thought about this. "And whatever that little part is, it probably looked more like me when it was my age."

"Good point." Bragger washed his goulash down with a gulp of milk and wiped his mouth with the back of his hand. "Our mission, then, is to scour Stuckey for pictures of Brett McGrew from when he was thirteen. Which shouldn't be a problem. One thing this town's got plenty of is pictures of McNet."

"Right." I unzipped my backpack and pulled out a crisp new spiral notebook.

Bragger looked at me. "Making a list?"

I nodded.

He crushed his empty milk carton. "I figured."

I opened the notebook to the first page and wrote *Places to Look for Pictures.*

"Uh-oh," Bragger groaned.

I looked up.

Duncan Webber, lunch tray in hand, hopeful smile stretched across his sweaty pink face, was headed straight toward Eddie and Russell. "Hey, guys." He gave them a little wave as he reached their table. Leaned over like he was going to set his tray down.

Eddie skewered him with a look. "That seat's saved."

Duncan blinked. "Oh. Okay." He scootched over to the next chair.

36

Russell shook his head. "Don't even think about it, Webber."

"Oh." Duncan swallowed. "Okay." He straightened up. Shot a panicked look around the lunchroom, looking for a seat that wasn't taken.

Bragger looked at me. I nodded and closed my notebook.

"Duncan." Bragger motioned his head toward our table. "You can sit with us."

Relief washed over Duncan's face. Followed by more panic as he realized where we were sitting. He eyed The Hulk, obviously weighing the pros and cons of eating lunch at the rickety beast. Hunger won out over social humiliation. He scrambled past Eddie and made his way toward an empty seat across from Bragger and me.

Unfortunately, this was Duncan we were talking about. Not a shining example of grace under pressure. He stumbled, and the next thing I saw was the napkin wad skidding free across the floor.

The Hulk teetered in space for a moment before the bent leg banged to the floor. My side of the table dropped like the heavy end of a seesaw. My tray slid south. I dropped my notebook and grabbed for it.

Duncan had been about to set his tray down when The Hulk lurched. His side of the table flew up. Knocked the tray out of Duncan's hands. The tray executed a perfect one-and-a-half gainer before—*whonk*—cracking my skull and sliding down my chest to my lap.

The clamor of the lunchroom ground to a dead stop.

37

Everyone turned to stare. At me, The Hulk, and Duncan's goulash.

One of the lunchroom ladies huffed over, her hairnet trembling in her rage.

"Were you boys raised in a barn?" She planted her beefy fists on her hips. Glared at the goulash dripping from my face. "If you can't be more careful, you'll find yourselves eating in the principal's office."

She thumped the high end of The Hulk down and shoved the napkin wad back under the bent leg. She straightened up. Shook a sausagelike finger at us.

"Lunch is a privilege. One you can lose." She slapped a wet dishrag onto The Hulk next to me. "Make sure you clean up every bit of it, mister."

A giggle erupted behind her. She turned toward Eddie's table.

"Did you have something to do with this, Mr. Poggemeyer?"

Eddie stopped giggling and gave her an offended, innocent look. "Me? No way." He shot a snarl my way. "I never have anything to do with that table."

The lunch lady wiped her hands on her apron and huffed back to the lunch line.

Duncan swallowed and sank into his chair. "I'm sorry, Kirby. I really am."

"It's okay." I picked a piece of macaroni from my eyelashes.

"No, it's not. Stuff like this always happens when I'm

around." Duncan glanced up at me. At his lunch plastered across my body. "And now I don't have anything to eat."

I sighed and slid my lunch tray across the table to him. "Have mine," I said. "I'm not really hungry anymore."

Eight

I was still picking goulash off my shirt when Bragger and I got to my house after school. I changed my clothes; then we holed up in my room, determined to find the perfect picture of Brett McGrew.

We started with my own collection. We spent that whole night and the next one rustling through scrapbooks, sports magazines, and souvenir game programs. We finally figured out I didn't have a single picture of Brett McGrew from before high school. But we also figured out where we *could* find pictures of him at that age: Stuckey Middle School, where, as luck would have it, Bragger and I were currently enrolled as seventh graders.

We snagged library passes during Social Studies the next day and combed through shelves of dusty yearbooks till we found the two from when Brett McGrew was in middle school. We hauled them down and made copies of every page Brett McGrew appeared on. That night we sorted through the Xeroxes, trying to find that one little part of thirteen-year-old Brett McGrew that looked like me.

We didn't find it. Or anything close. Not in the Xeroxes or in the middle school trophy cases we scoured after school the next day.

Which was disappointing, of course, but not as disappointing as I would have expected. Taking action, *doing* something, even something that so far wasn't working out, was better than drifting through each day, waiting for something to happen.

"Besides," I told Bragger on Friday, when he came over to spend the night, "we've got three months left before the KU game, and we haven't begun to exhaust our research possibilities." I consulted the list of *Places to Look for Pictures* in my notebook. "We've still got the public library downtown, where they store back issues of the Stuckey *Full Court Press*. There's surely pictures of thirteen-year-old Brett in that mess. And the trophy case at the high school. And the Internet, of course. The possibilities just stretch out ahead of us."

And those possibilities were a lot more fun to think about than my other problem. The one I hadn't mentioned to Bragger. The one I tried not to mention to myself. Because this was it: What if Brett McGrew already knew I was his son?

And didn't care?

I wasn't sure any plan we came up with would cover that.

Nine

The older folks in town like to tell about the night Brett McGrew was born. They say the sky was clear and the moon was full, a moon that lay low on the horizon, big and round and orange, like a basketball. A giant basketball shining down on Stuckey. They say they remember it just like it was yesterday.

Grandma says those folks conveniently started remembering that moon after the coaching staff at the University of Kansas first took notice of Brett McGrew. McNet went to KU basketball camp the summer after his seventh-grade year. At the end of the week, when his parents came to pick him up, the head coach pulled them aside and told them they had a budding basketball star on their hands. He told them he was going to keep an eye on young Brett. He told them not to be surprised if the University of Kansas offered Brett McGrew a basketball scholarship when he got old enough. Which, of course, is exactly what they did.

And which, of course, explains why every boy in the entire seventh grade, all twelve of us, signed up for basketball. Eleven of those boys were hoping a basketball moon had been lying low in the sky, unnoticed, the night they were born. That they were budding young basketball stars waiting to be discovered. That the KU coaching staff would start recruiting them during their seventh-grade year, just like Brett McGrew. Especially now that the team was traveling all the way to Lawrence to be on TV with McNet during a KU game.

Me, I just wanted to fade into the metal folding chair farthest down the bench from Coach and stay there till basketball season was over, with nobody noticing my basketball skills—or embarrassing lack of basketball skills—at all. My best strategy was to look confident riding the bench. To appear as if I'd know exactly what I was doing if I ever got to play.

And pray Coach was sane enough to never actually put me in.

The first day of practice, I marched into the locker room armed with a gym bag, roll-on deodorant, and a brand-new pair of McNet XJ7 Jammers from the JCPenney over in Great Bend. The shoes were a gift from my grandmother, who, when she thought I wasn't looking, also bought Ace bandages, an ice pack, and a quart-size jar of professional-strength deep-heating rub. I think she was less confident in my athletic ability than she let on.

The other guys were already there, bragging and swaggering. But I was ready for it. I'd been practicing. I'd worked out a pretty smooth high five, and I knew I could count on Bragger for at least one good chest bump. Plus, I'd spent twenty minutes that morning in front of the bathroom mirror perfecting my one-handed, at-the-waist fist clutch—"Yes! He scores!"

I dangled my Jammers casually over one shoulder, raised my hand in flawless high-five form, and slapped and jabbed my way across the locker room. Duncan Webber punched my shoulder. Manning Reece air-boxed me to my locker. And Bragger was good for the chest bump. So good, I think he dislocated my ribcage.

But I didn't care. I stood there sock-footed on the clammy cement and took it all in. Clanking lockers. Flying sweat socks. Toxic sneaker fumes mingled with the aroma of industrial-strength disinfectant. If I didn't think about it too hard, I could almost believe I belonged here: Kirby Nickel, Superjock.

Right. More like, Kirby Nickel, Kid Who Breaks Out in Hives Lacing up His Gym Shoes.

I peeled off my jeans and T-shirt. And casually tugged on the legs of my undershorts so they'd cover as much skin as possible. I'd been wearing boxer briefs ever since I'd started seventh-grade P.E. because I sure didn't need a bunch of other guys staring at my butt every day. At the enormous, humiliating, heart-shaped pink birthmark on the back of my leg, right where my thigh met my butt cheek. Boxer briefs were the perfect solution—long enough to cover my legs and snug enough not to flop around when I moved. I tugged on them again just to be sure.

I wriggled into my practice clothes, then hunkered on the bench in front of my locker and pulled on my Jammers.

Practice went about as well as any of us expected. We were, after all, the Stuckey seventh-grade basketball team.

Missing the basket was clearly our best talent. Coach spent most of his time blowing his whistle and assigning laps. By the time practice was over, we'd run around the gym at least 150 times, which, by my calculations, equaled roughly twelve miles, which, if we'd been running out on the highway, would've taken us all the way to Whipple and back. We filed into the locker room, our sweat-soaked practice clothes clinging to bodies too exhausted for even a half-hearted high five.

Coach marched in behind us.

"You think you worked hard, don't you?" he barked. "You think you can take your showers now and scurry on home to your mommies. Well, you got one more thing to take care of. You gotta elect yourselves a team captain." He narrowed his eyes. "Think long and hard about who you pick. Your captain is your team representative. The face you show to the world. You pick somebody who's not up to the job, what does that tell the world?"

The truth, probably. But I didn't say that.

Coach looked us up and down for a long moment, then strode into his office and swung the door shut behind him. We stood there for a minute, watching the miniblinds in his office windows rattle against the glass. Then Eddie stepped forward. Of course. "I think we can take care of this pretty fast." He snapped the waistband of his sweaty shorts. "It's obvious who should be team captain. And as captain"—he sauntered toward the shower room—"I believe the first shower is mine."

"Whoa." Bragger stepped out into the aisle to block his way. "Hold onto your panties there, Gertrude. You can't just appoint yourself captain. You heard Coach. We need to give this serious thought. We need to take nominations, discuss each candidate's strengths, and vote."

Bragger turned to face the rest of the team. The jack-o'-lantern grin stretched across his face, and I knew trouble was on its way. Trouble that undoubtedly included me. I swear, if Bragger and I hadn't been cousins, I wonder if we'd even be friends. Friends you can pick. Family you're just stuck with.

"For our first and, as I'm sure you'll all agree, most qualified candidate, I'm nominating"—Bragger flung his arm around my shoulders—"Kirby Nickel."

"Kirby Nickel?" I stared at him.

"Kirby Nickel?" Eddie stared at him too. "How do you figure?"

I didn't care how he figured. "Look, Bragger, I don't want—"

Bragger clamped a hand over my mouth. "Trust me, Kirb," he muttered in my ear.

He puffed up his chest and gazed from player to player. "Our captain must go above and beyond the call of basketball. He must put the team's needs ahead of his own." Bragger's voice quivered with emotion, just like Reverend Wesley Jack Wooten's, the TV evangelist on Channel 7. "Who here is willing to make that sacrifice? To put the team's needs above his own comfort? Be honest now. Who among us is willing to lead this team no matter how much it hurts?"

"Hurts?" said Duncan. "I don't want to get hurt."

"Me, neither," said Russell. "I thought the captain just had to shake hands with the other team's captain before games and stand next to Coach for yearbook pictures."

Bragger nodded. "That's what a lot of people think, Russell." He gave the team a sad, sympathetic smile. "But there's more to it than that. There's leadership. Courage. Honesty. Think about it. Who had the guts to attempt a spinning layup in front of the school board? Yes, he fell on his face, and yes, he knocked the wind out of himself. The point is, he wasn't afraid. He wasn't afraid to try, and he wasn't afraid to face Coach's fury. Kirby Nickel is not afraid to endure pain for the sake of his team."

"Yes, I am, Bragger," I hissed. "I am very afraid."

"Kirby Nickel knows what his team needs."

"No, I don't, Bragger. No. I. Don't."

"Kirby Nickel will lead our team to victory." Bragger grabbed my wrist and pulled it straight up in the air, like a prizefighter who'd scored a knockout. "He's got my vote for team captain. Who's with me?"

"Me!" Duncan's hand shot up. I'm not sure he was voting for me or voting to keep his own sorry self out of danger.

One by one the hands went up. Bragger had converted the nonbelievers. And I, Kirby Nickel, the clumsiest kid in the gym, was elected captain of the Stuckey seventh-grade Prairie Dogs.

Bragger was still holding my wrist, and now I yanked it, and him, to the side. "You just elected me to a whole heap of trouble, you know that? Do you know what Coach is going to do when he finds out who his captain is?"

"I bet he'll be surprised."

"Surprised?"

An image flashed into my brain: Coach, the way he looked after my spinning belly flop. Face squinched into a burning snarl. Purple vein in his neck pulsing with rage. Fists clenched so tight his biceps strained against the sleeves of his sweatshirt. Biceps that were bigger around than my entire flimsy body.

"Oh, he'll be surprised," I said. "He'll probably hemorrhage, he'll be so surprised. I'll be doing a fair amount of bleeding myself, what with his big, meaty fists clamped around my throat all season long. What were you thinking?"

Bragger looked at me for a long moment. "I don't get you, Kirby. Every kid in the world is dying to be captain of *something*. But you, you'd rather be the guy who gets picked last choosing up sides." His shoulders slumped. The Wesley Jack Wooten voice was gone. "Fine. Go ahead and be mad. You won't think it's so awful when you're scrunched up next to Brett McGrew at the KU game, grinning like an idiot at the TV cameras."

"What are you talking about?"

He shook his head. "For such a smart kid, you are unbelievably slow sometimes. Who do you *think* is going to be hanging out with McNet? Not Eddie or Russell. And certainly not Duncan." He flung his arm toward the team. "None of those guys. Because they aren't the captain. You are. And even if it doesn't mean anything to you, it probably does to Brett McGrew."

He ambled over to where the rest of the team stood watching. Waiting. Sweaty red faces looking to their captain to make his next move.

I blinked. Brett McGrew. Standing next to Brett McGrew. Maybe even talking to him. In actual conversation. All because I was the captain of the basketball team. And Bragger . . .

I glanced at him. He had his foot up on the bench and was tying and retying his shoestrings into a sturdy, even bow, careful not to look at me.

. . . Bragger had figured this all out before we ever got here. He probably started planning it the minute I told him Brett McGrew was my father. He'd cooked up his own surprise Step Three of The Plan: Get Kirby elected captain against his will.

Still, what if Bragger was right? What if I *could* be the team captain? What if somewhere, deep inside, I had it in me?

I did have some admirable qualities, after all. I was conscientious and responsible. And smart. I got very good grades, especially in math. I kicked butt in math. I also kept my room fairly tidy and brushed my teeth twice a day without being told to.

And what was that other stuff Bragger said I had?

Leadership? Courage? Okay, so leadership and courage might be stretching it. But he also mentioned honesty, and I certainly do have that. Mainly because I am not a very good liar. Still, I *am* honest, and that counts.

It had to. Otherwise all I had going for me was mathematics and good personal hygiene.

Ten

My first job as team captain was to go find the janitor to unlock the supply closet. It had taken one middle-school basketball team exactly six minutes and twenty-seven seconds to turn a moderately scummy locker room into a festering biohazard, and if I was going in, I needed heavy artillery: mop, plunger, industrial-strength deodorizing cleanser. And rubber gloves. No way was I picking up their fungus-infested towels with my bare hands.

My second job was to give Coach the results of our election.

I made sure the janitor was still around when I did it. I figured I'd need somebody to unclog the toilet after Coach tried to flush me down.

But Coach surprised me.

He didn't growl or snarl or clench his fists or make one move toward turning me into a human swirly cone. He just pooched his lips and looked at me, eyes narrowed.

"Team captain. Huh." He looked me up and down. "You're not exactly athletic, but you're bright. I can't see you doing anything too stupid." He leaned closer till his eyes were level with mine. "You won't do anything stupid, will you, Nickel?"

I swallowed. "No, sir."

"Good." He nodded and ambled out of the locker room.

The janitor followed him.

I rinsed out the mop bucket, flipped off the lights, and trudged through the empty gym by myself. Bragger had offered to wait for me, but I told him no, go on home, I was team captain now and had certain responsibilities.

The truth was, I couldn't blame him for coming up with a secret Step Three. I'd devised my own Step Three, and I hadn't seen fit to tell Bragger about it.

Of course, my Step Three didn't put anybody else's personal safety in jeopardy. My Step Three only involved getting people to do more of what they liked doing anyway: talk about Brett McGrew. My Step Three was to find out what kind of person Brett McGrew was, to see if he was the kind of guy who could go around knowing he had a son and not do anything about it. To see if maybe the reason my mom never told anyone Brett McGrew was my father was because Brett McGrew didn't want to *be* my father.

Which was why I didn't go straight home after practice. I scrunched my jacket up around my ears, leaned into the wind, and headed to the Double Dribble.

Warm cafe air wrapped around me when I walked through the door. I wound my way through the tables and scooted onto the stool at the end of the counter.

Mrs. Snodgrass filled a glass with Coke and set it in front of me. "Where'd you lose Bragger?" She reached under the counter for a straw.

"No place." I dropped my backpack onto the floor. "Bragger and I don't always do everything together."

"Really." Mrs. Snodgrass looked at me. Her eyebrows were two thick black crayon marks carefully drawn across the bald ridges above her eyes. She raised them now, surprised. "I don't believe I've ever seen either one of you doing anything apart."

I shrugged—casually, I hoped—and peeled the paper from my straw. I didn't have anybody to throw it at, so I set it next to my Coke.

Mrs. Snodgrass had the radio tuned to her usual country-and-western station, and now she started filling up saltshakers, sashaying around the restaurant in time with Garth Brooks. I could hear her husband, Mr. Snodgrass, clanking dishes around in the kitchen, but the afternoon coffee drinkers had all gone home, and the supper crowd hadn't come in yet. So except for me and Mrs. Snodgrass, the restaurant was empty.

"Hey, Mrs. Snodgrass," I said. Still casual. "How well did you know Brett McGrew? You know, back when he was in high school?"

Mrs. Snodgrass unscrewed a saltshaker lid. "As well as most folks, I guess. Went to all his games, of course. And he stopped in here pretty regular. Him and his daddy used to come in on Saturday mornings for breakfast. Started when Brett was real little, and they kept coming in every Saturday till he went away to college. Even after that, they'd still have breakfast here sometimes when Brett was down from KU. He said nobody in Lawrence knew how to fix decent biscuits and gravy, so he had to load up on them whenever he was home." She set the newly filled saltshaker back on the table and raised a crayon mark at me. "Why?"

"Oh. No reason," I said. "I was just wondering what he was like. As a person. You know, since I'll be meeting him and all when the team goes to KU."

Mrs. Snodgrass nodded. "I can understand that." She picked up another saltshaker. "But I don't think you have anything to worry about. Brett was always a nice kid. That kind of talent would've turned most people arrogant, I guess, but not Brett. He didn't get rowdy in here like some of the kids, putting mustard in the ketchup bottles and loosening the sugar lids. He was polite. Haven't seen him in years, though. Not since he started making all that money and built his parents that big house out in Arizona." She screwed the lid back on the saltshaker. "Hope the NBA didn't ruin him."

Yeah. Me, too.

I finished my Coke, counted out the money to pay for it, and left it on the counter. I grabbed my backpack and tromped outside, into the wind and the growing darkness. I pulled my spiral notebook from my backpack. It wasn't quite as crisp and new, now that it was flecked with goulash stains. I scraped a dried chunk off the cover, flipped past my list of *Places to Look for Pictures*, and set the notebook on top of the big, square *Full Court Press* vending machine that stood outside the cafe.

Wind whipped at the pages. I weighted them down with my algebra book and wrote *What I Know about Brett McGrew* at the top of the page. Then I listed everything Mrs. Snodgrass had told me:

Not arrogant
Not rowdy
Good manners
Likes biscuits and gravy

I looked at my list. It didn't help much. I'd know what to fix if he ever dropped by for breakfast, but I wasn't any closer to knowing how he felt about kids.
Especially his own.

Eleven

Bragger wrenched his tail loose, and the heavy metal door banged shut. We stood there for a stunned second, huddled inside our musty prairie dog costume, waiting to be tossed out of the high school—again—but nobody looked our way. The music was thudding so loud, nobody'd heard us when we clanked in the side entrance.

"Try to blend in," Bragger hissed in my ear. "Walk like you're in high school."

We had tried to get in the legal way. We'd sacrificed our Coke at the Double Dribble and raced over to the high school as soon as practice was over. Bragger had secretly borrowed his dad's no-flash camera and brand-new, auto-crisp zoom lens. We figured we'd casually snap a few shots of the Brett McGrew photos in the high school trophy case and hope one of those photos showed a piece of Brett McGrew that looked like me.

As usual, we figured wrong. The assistant principal had been stationed inside the front doors, his suit jacket pushed back behind the bony fists he'd planted on his hips. Bragger and I had barely gotten the front door open before he turned us around again and headed us back outside. Punky little middle school kids had no business on high school property. We were up to no good. He could tell just by looking at us.

Fortunately, Bragger had noticed a flyer for the Halloween dance taped to the door. He snatched it down and tucked it under his coat as the vice principal shoved us out of his school.

Which is how we ended up inside the prairie dog.

The costume was Grandma's. She'd been the back half of the mascot at all the football and basketball games when she was in high school. The costume had been stored in the attic, wrapped in old sheets, for longer than I could remember, and when Bragger and I suddenly found ourselves in need of a Halloween costume that would cover us up so completely nobody would guess who we were, I immediately thought of the prairie dog.

We hauled it down from the attic and cleaned it up as best we could with a lint brush and a can of air freshener. Grandma muttered something about us getting a little too old for trick-or-treating, and we didn't argue with her. Better to let her think we were immature babies looking to score free chocolate than to admit we'd turned to a life of crime.

The worst part, the part that almost made me confess our crimes even before we'd committed any, was that even though Grandma thought we were immature, she seemed proud that we wanted to be immature wearing her prairie dog. She dragged the vacuum cleaner out of the hall closet and helped us suck the cobwebs off with her drapery attachment.

"Sure has been a good old prairie dog." She ran her hand over its mangy ears. "He needs a little cleaning up, but he's still in good shape. Solid." She rapped the prairie dog's head with her knuckles. "He's served three generations of our family well."

I looked up from the lint I was removing. "Three?"

Grandma nodded. "You, me, and your mother. She wore it a time or two when she was in school."

"She did?" I looked down at the fuzz accumulated on my lint brush. I'd been throwing that fuzz away. Right in the trash can. Not realizing that it might have come off one of my mother's sweaters or something.

And then I had another thought. This was a costume built for two.

"Who'd she wear it with?" I said.

Grandma shrugged. "Oh, I don't know. Different ones." She dragged the vacuum around so she could suction decades of dust from the prairie dog's back end. "Friends of hers. They were all taller than her, of course, and she ended up in back, just like I always did."

"Taller?" I said. "Like how tall?"

Grandma frowned at me and dropped the tail. "I don't know, Kirby. Tall enough to be the front end of a prairie dog."

She powered the vacuum cleaner off, wound the cord around the handle, and lugged it back to the hall closet.

I thunked Bragger in the arm. "Did you hear that? My mother wore this with somebody who was *taller than her*."

Bragger nodded. "Yeah."

"Yeah? Think about it. Who do we know who went to school with my mom who was taller than her?"

"Everyone."

"But who in particular?"

"Everyone."

"Okay. But who was *really* taller than her?"

Bragger rolled his eyes. "Brett McGrew. Brett McGrew was really taller than your mother. Brett McGrew must've worn this costume with her. In fact, Brett McGrew probably asked her to the Sweetheart Dance right here in this flea-bitten mound of fur. Is that what you want to hear?"

Yes, actually, it was.

And now here we were, hunkered down inside that same flea-bitten mound of fur, breathing three generations of dust and mildew as we waddled toward the high school trophy case.

And possibly toward our doom.

Music blasted from the cafeteria. Cowboys, fortune-tellers, and somebody dressed like a giant zit flocked toward it. But the trophy case was on the other side of the building, down the hallway, around the corner by the home ec room, past the office, and into the front lobby.

We circled a gang of belly dancers clustered outside the girls' bathroom and headed toward the darkness. Casually. Not running. Not panicking. Not attracting the attention of suspicious vice principals. Just your ordinary, everyday prairie dog, shuffling away from a party.

We rounded the corner by the home ec room. Except for a far-off glow coming from around the corner at the other end, the hall was pitch-black. An ax murderer could've been waving a big shiny ax in my face, and I wouldn't have seen him. I gripped the camera and set off through the darkness. Bragger shuffled along behind. We reached the far end. I veered to the side and hugged the wall.

I slid one side of my big prairie dog head around the corner and peered through the eyehole. The glow I'd seen was coming from the lobby, from the display lights in the trophy case.

And in front of the trophy case—

—stood Coach.

"*Ulgp!*" I strangled a yelp and pulled my prairie dog head back. Fast.

And almost dropped the camera. I grabbed for it. My finger hit the button, taking a picture of who knew what. I gave a silent prayer of gratitude that it was a no-flash camera. And waited for a horrified minute to see if Coach had heard the click.

"What?" Bragger whispered. "The vice principal?"

"Worse," I hissed. "Coach."

"Coach? What's *he* doing here?"

"I don't know, Bragger. I didn't have my head poked out there long enough to find out."

"Well, stick it out again and see."

I took a deep breath and inched my prairie dog head past the corner. I felt like some kind of spy: Kirby Nickel, alias James Bond. Cleverly disguised as a giant rodent. I aimed my eyehole at Coach.

He stood perfectly still, his back to me, staring into the trophy case. His arms were splayed out on the case above him, his forehead pressed against it. His breath huffed out in a foggy circle on the glass.

At first I thought he was staring at the Brett McGrew stuff. The trophies and medals. The retired number 5 jersey. The poster-size cutout photo of McNet tipping in the winning basket at the state championship his senior year.

That's what most people stare at. You can't help yourself, everything's so big and shiny.

But Coach was off to one side, where the team photos were a little smaller. And a lot dustier. The medals were tarnished, the ribbons faded, and the trophies weren't polished to a blinding sheen. One of the display lights was burnt out, and that whole section of the trophy case fell under the shadow of the giant Brett McGrew cutout.

Coach snorted and pushed back from the glass, and I could finally see what he'd been staring at: an old team picture. Fluffy-haired players in skin-tight shorts.

Coach stood there rubbing his bristly chin. Finally he tapped his finger on the glass, almost like he was saying good-bye, and started to walk away. He stopped at the Brett McGrew cutout. Stared at it for a long moment.

He shook his head, gave another little snort, and clanked through the double doors on the other side of the lobby.

"He's gone," I said.

We trundled around the corner, to the big, shiny Brett

61

McGrew display. I wedged the camera into my eyehole and snapped pictures of the trophies, the medals, the jersey, the team photos, the newspaper clippings. I took three pictures of the giant cutout from various directions, just in case looking at it from a different angle made it look more like me.

I backed Bragger up so I could snap a picture of the entire display. The camera clicked and made a little whirring noise.

"Out of film," I said. "Let's go."

We started to turn around and trundle back the way we had come. But then we heard voices. And keys jingling. A door creaked open, and lights flashed on around the corner. Voices again; then somebody laughed.

"The vice principal," Bragger hissed.

"In the office," I whispered back.

For a second, we just stood there. We couldn't go back. And we sure couldn't stay where we were. The only way out was the door Coach had disappeared through. I dragged Bragger across the lobby and eased the door open. I squeezed through, Bragger fishtailed around behind me, and I eased the door shut.

And there was Coach. Again. This time dribbling a basketball in the nearly dark gymnasium. I pressed Bragger and me and the prairie dog into the little space at the end of the bleachers. And peered out through my eyeholes. A shaft of moonlight shone through the windows above the bleachers, spotlighting the basket at the far end of the court. Coach dribbled in place, then drove toward the basket. When he reached it, he took one last step, pushed off, and leaped. Up and around and around again.

Th-bumpf.

The ball hit the backboard and swished through the net.

Brett McGrew's famous spinning layup.

Executed perfectly.

Twelve

"A spinning layup?" Bragger splatted through a puddle. "Kinda like Brett McGrew?"

"No," I said. "*Exactly* like Brett McGrew. He never missed. Not once."

We'd stayed there in the gym, squashed against the bleachers, until Coach finally got tired and left. Then we scrambled across the court, still stuffed into the costume, and out the side door at the other end.

Now we were headed home, Bragger's dad's no-flash auto-crisp camera stuffed up under the prairie dog for protection. It was drizzling, like it did every Halloween, with the wind spitting rain at us, and I couldn't risk getting the camera wet. My whole future rested on that one roll of film.

I veered off the sidewalk. Bragger slogged along behind, splashing mud up the back of my legs. We cut through the side yard and crunched down my driveway.

"You know," said Bragger, "Coach must be taking this whole retiring-the-jersey thing more seriously than he's letting on. I mean, he acts like meeting Brett McGrew is no big deal, but then there he is, practicing McNet's moves in the gym."

"Yeah," I said. "Iron Man Mike Armstrong: secret Brett McGrew fan. Who knew?"

We clomped up the back steps, through the porch, and into the house. The kitchen was empty. I could hear Grandma in the front room, handing out bite-size Snickers and pretending to be scared of a three-foot-tall vampire.

Bragger wriggled out of the back end of the costume. I lifted the prairie dog head off my own head. Or at least, I tried to lift it. I got the shoulder part about as high as my throat before it caught on something and snapped back. About strangled me.

I reached up under the prairie dog head and found the problem: a piece of wire that had gotten hooked on the little zipper-pull thingy on the front of my sweatshirt. I poked it out and pulled off the mangy prairie dog head.

A small metal disk clanked to the floor.

"Hey." I picked it up and held it up to the light. "Look at this."

Bragger squinted. "Looks like a medal. Like from a letter jacket or something."

"Yeah." I scrubbed it across my jeans to get the dust off. "Whoa."

"What?" Bragger leaned closer to get a better look.

"There's a basketball on the front. And look what it says: *Great Plains League Champions, Boys' Varsity Basketball.*"

Bragger took the medal. He studied the front, then flipped it over. "The year's engraved on the back. Wow, this sucker's old. What is that, like eighteen years ago?"

"Eighteen years ago?" I plucked the medal from Bragger's fingers.

And stared at the date. Stared at the basketball medal glimmering in the palm of my hand. For a moment, I couldn't move. If this had been a movie instead of my pitiful ordinary life, light would've shone down, orchestra music would've swelled, and Bragger and I would've stared at each other in slow motion, stunned by the hugeness of the moment.

"Eighteen years ago," I said, my voice barely a whisper. "Brett McGrew would've been a freshman in high school." I looked up. "Do you realize what this means?"

"No," said Bragger, obviously not stunned by the hugeness of the moment. "But I'm sure you'll tell me."

"It means Brett McGrew was inside this prairie dog head."

He looked at me sideways. "It does?"

"Yeah. Brett McGrew wore this costume with my mother. Think about it. My mom's the back of the prairie dog, and Brett McGrew's the front, because he's taller. And he's wearing his letter jacket, and this little wire thing gets caught on his medal, just like it got caught on my sweatshirt, only he doesn't realize it, just like I didn't at first, and when he pulls it off, he rips the medal off, too. And it gets stuck. Only he doesn't notice. And Brett McGrew's freshman-year league championship medal stays right here in my mother's prairie dog head for eighteen years."

"Lucky thing you came along to find it," said Bragger.

"You're right. I didn't even think about that. Eighteen

years later, I come along, looking for evidence that will prove who Brett McGrew really is, who *I* really am, and I find his medal. Only you know what? It's not luck. It's more like, like fate. Like it was supposed to happen."

"When you grow up, Kirby, you ought to think about writing soap operas. Seriously. You'd be good at it. Stuff like this happens a lot on Grandma's stories."

I looked at him. "This is not Grandma's stories, Bragger. This is a basketball medal from Brett McGrew's freshman year that got stuck inside a prairie dog my mother used to wear. That's a fact. I didn't make it up."

"Okay. Don't get mad." He held his hands up. "All I'm saying is, there were probably twelve guys on that basketball team. Twelve guys who got medals. And eleven of them weren't Brett McGrew. That's all I'm saying. I'm just trying to be, you know, the voice of reason."

Oh, yeah. Bragger Barnes, voice of reason.

We hauled the prairie dog up the back stairway and set it in the tub in the upstairs bathroom so it could dry out. I stashed the medal in my underwear drawer, inside one of my lucky Jayhawk sweat socks.

Because I knew what I had to do with it. I would take it with me to Lawrence, where I'd personally present it to Brett McGrew. After all these years, he'd probably given up hope of ever finding it again. He probably didn't even let himself think about it anymore because the memory was too painful.

And I, Kirby Nickel, would be the one to take that pain

away. I would reunite Brett McGrew with his very first championship medal. He'd be so grateful he'd probably want to adopt me on the spot.

Which would make it a whole lot easier for me to tell him I was already his son.

Thirteen

The wild October wind swirled into a chill November blast. It whistled through town, plastering bits of litter flat against the playground fence and whipping the flags above the post office into a wind-beaten frenzy.

Something was whipping the town's good citizens into a frenzy, too, but it wasn't the wind.

I got my first whiff of it Monday after practice. Grandma was at the kitchen table sorting through mail when I got home. I banged through the back door and dropped my backpack onto a chair. Grandma didn't look up. Just handed me a folded-up newspaper article.

"Sports column," she said. "My cousin Mildred up in Tonganoxie sent it. Clipped it out of Sunday's Kansas City *Star*."

I unfolded it. JAYHAWK FLIES HOME, read the headline. Then in smaller print underneath, *Kansas's Favorite Son Returns to College to See Jersey Retired.*

It was more than your ordinary sports column. It was half of the front page of the sports section, plus two pages on the inside. It documented Brett McGrew's entire career, from Stuckey High School to MVP of last year's NBA championship game. In color. With pictures.

I looked up at Grandma. "This was really nice of your cousin."

"Huh." Grandma was studying the water bill. "Not as nice as you might think. Mildred's always felt a little superior, living as close as she does to Kansas City."

I scootched into a kitchen chair and smoothed the clipping out in front of me.

The column started with the usual stuff: college feats, NBA feats, awards, stats, records. Nothing I hadn't read a thousand times before. But I didn't mind. I'd read it again. Another thousand times probably.

But then I got to a section about Brett McGrew's humble beginnings:

> Brett McGrew's basketball career started in the most unlikely of places: Stuckey, Kansas, population 334. It started the day Brett McGrew's father nailed a backboard to the side of his barn and held three-year-old Brett up to drop a basketball through the hoop.

I stopped reading, almost afraid to see what came next. This section of this article might be the very thing I needed. Exactly what I'd been searching for. The last crucial piece of evidence. Something from his years in Stuckey that would prove he was my father.

Not that I actually thought it would say, "And now that he's attained such success on the court, McNet's fondest wish is to connect with the son he left behind in his hometown." But I did think it might mention something I could use. Maybe about the people who helped Brett McGrew get from Stuckey to national acclaim. Like, say, his high school basketball coach. Or his high school teammates. Or maybe his girlfriend. Maybe the article said something about my mother.

I glanced up at Grandma. She was flipping through the JCPenney sale flyer, not paying any attention to me. I pulled the paper closer and started reading again:

> Since Brett McGrew's days as a high school player, Stuckey has hitched its reputation to its most famous—or should I say, *only* famous—son. No matter where you go in this one-stoplight town, from the water tower to the lone gas station, you're bombarded by signs, scoreboards, T-shirts, coffee mugs, matchbook covers, and bumper stickers, all proclaiming Stuckey as the "Basketball Capital of Kansas." Which begs the question: Could this tiny wind-blown corner of the prairie really be the basketball capital of the entire state?
>
> A glance through the Kansas high school record books provides an answer. While it's true that the Stuckey Prairie Dogs have played for the Kansas state high school championship four times—all four years Brett McGrew was in school, with McNet

leading his team to victories in three of those games—Stuckey hasn't been to the playoffs before or since. Want to know how pathetic their record is? The town is sending its seventh-grade team to watch Brett McGrew's jersey retirement, and the Stuckey seventh graders haven't won a game in three years.

It's also true that, to this day, players from Stuckey hold the Kansas high school records for most career points, rebounds, steals, blocked shots, and free throws. But guess who holds them? Yep. Except for most steals, held by some obscure Stuckey guard nobody's ever heard of, Brett McGrew holds every single one of those records.

The verdict? The town's reputation rests on one guy, one amazing, legendary player: Brett "McNet" McGrew. Without him, Stuckey would have no claim to the title "Basketball Capital of Kansas." It would more likely be "The Forgotten Armpit of Kansas." But of course, that wouldn't sell as many bumper stickers.

Armpit? I blinked. Wow.

I must've rustled the paper or something, because Grandma peered over her bifocals at me. "Guess you got to the part Mildred likes," she said.

★

Unfortunately, Grandma and I weren't the only ones in Stuckey to get their hands on a copy of that sports column.

Within twenty-four hours, the Forgotten Armpit of Kansas had replaced Lloyd Metcalf's fancy new combine as the main topic of conversation at the Double Dribble. Mrs. Snodgrass had more coffee business that week than she'd had all fall, although she was losing some of her customers to the periodical section of the public library, which had suddenly become one of the most popular spots in town. Folks clogged the aisle, waiting their turn to read the library's lone copy of the Sunday Kansas City *Star*.

Well. Mrs. Zimmer wasn't about to stand by and let a big-city paper like the *Star* sully the town's good name. No, sir. She fired off a letter to the editor, demanding a full apology. Then she marched down to the library and demanded that the librarian remove the offending sports section from the Sunday issue.

The librarian refused, of course. Even here in Stuckey we've heard of freedom of the press. But Mrs. Zimmer wasn't one to let a little thing like civil liberties stand in her way. She marched over to the periodical section herself and snapped the tattered sports section from the ninety-seven-year-old hands of Mr. Homer Hawkins. She tucked it in her purse and marched out of the library. "This article is good for only one thing," she said as she rattled out the door. "Lighting a fire in my fireplace."

"And she did it, too," said Duncan. "Burned it up as soon as she got home."

73

Duncan was always a reliable source of information, what with his mother running the only beauty parlor in town.

"Didn't do her much good, though," Duncan added. "Somebody Xeroxed that column first thing Monday morning. Copies have been floating around town all week. My mom's got a whole stack of them by her cash register."

Within twenty-four hours, everybody from here to Dodge City had heard that the seventh-grade team from the Armpit of Kansas was headed to Lawrence to honor Brett McGrew.

And Mrs. Zimmer was more upset about it than anybody at the beauty parlor realized.

Fourteen

The Wichita paper ran a small story about the "Forgotten Armpit" column on its inside pages, and a morning disc jockey at one of the radio stations over in Hutch kept playing a recording of a big armpit fart over and over all week long.

But other than that, the hubbub pretty much died down.

We thought.

Friday we bounded into the gym—the Stuckey seventh-grade Prairie Dogs, decked out in our practice duds. The hairs on my arms stood up as we milled around the ball cart waiting for Coach.

Because we were not alone.

Mrs. Zimmer and Mr. Dobbs were once again seated in the first row of bleachers. Mr. Dobbs leaned forward, elbows on his knees, staring at the toes of his work boots. Mrs. Zimmer sat up straight and tall, her laser eyes burning holes in the team.

"What are *they* doing here?" Bragger whispered.

I shrugged.

The locker room door banged open. Coach marched into the gym and stopped in front of us, clipboard in one fist, whistle in the other. He studied Mrs. Zimmer. He shook his head, glared at the team, and barked, "Is this a tea party, or are you people here to play basketball?"

Coach led us through stretches and wind sprints, pivots and passing drills. Then we faced off in a scrimmage.

And I didn't think we did too bad, considering that we were, well, us. Bragger made two baskets. So did Eddie. Russell sank one. I even hit the rim a couple of times. We got only two balls stuck behind the backboard, and we kept our nosebleed total down to one.

Mine.

It was Duncan's sweat glands that finally did us in.

Duncan is a sweaty kid. No way around it. When he gets to running up and down a basketball court, he turns into a regular fountain. And he didn't even have a T-shirt on to sop up the excess. We were playing shirts and skins, and Duncan, regrettably, was a skin.

Eddie rebounded one of Bragger's missed three-pointers and passed to Russell. At that same moment, Duncan tripped and, purely by accident, picked off the pass.

After snagging the basketball like that, Duncan wasn't taking any chances. He hugged the ball tight to his bare, lathered-up belly and wrapped both arms around it so Russell couldn't slap it away. Then, in what could've been an amazing move, Duncan faked to his left, broke to his right, and drove in for the easy basket.

Easy. *Right.* In somebody else's universe.

You could tell right away Duncan was headed for trouble. Direct contact with his armpits hadn't helped the ball any, plus Duncan's stomach is not as lean and firm as it could be.

He bounded toward the basket. His right hand flew out, ready to dribble.

But the ball stayed put.

Duncan's sweat had caused such a suction between his skin and the leather of the basketball that for a split second, the ball remained stuck to his belly button. Just long enough for Duncan to take two steps and look really confused. Then the ball tore loose with a big *slurp* and bounced out of bounds.

Coach blew his whistle and called Duncan for traveling.

Mrs. Zimmer slammed her notebook shut and stood up.

I was still standing on the sidelines with toilet paper up my nose, so I saw her first. She marched across the gym, her sturdy brown shoes squeaking against the wood floor. Mr. Dobbs clomped along behind. They stopped in front of Coach.

Coach glared. Mrs. Zimmer glared back. Like two gunslingers facing off at high noon.

Mrs. Zimmer drew first. Her weapon: the black notebook. She whipped it open. "Mr. Armstrong, I believe you know why we're here. We need to determine whether your trip to the University of Kansas should, in fact, be canceled."

I think she was trying to whisper, but Mrs. Zimmer has a voice that can split atoms. The word "canceled" sliced right through the gym. The players stopped scrambling around the court and turned their full huffing-and-puffing attention to Mrs. Zimmer, Mr. Dobbs, and Coach.

The basketball rolled toward the sidelines. I grabbed it before it rolled into the wrestling mats.

"Despite what that sports column implied," Mrs. Zimmer was saying, "Stuckey is a basketball town. We have a strong basketball tradition. And you, Mr. Armstrong, are simply not keeping up the tradition."

"Tradition?" Coach's cheek muscles were clenched so tight they were quivering. "Tradition? Let me tell you something about tradition, Mrs. Zimmer. I was on the—"

"No," said Mrs. Zimmer. "Let me tell *you*, Mr. Armstrong. We hired you because you assured us you could turn this basketball team around. You promised you could develop a winning strategy. And you convinced us, against our better judgment, to send the seventh graders to Lawrence. But from what I've just seen, you haven't developed a winning strategy. You have no strategy at all. These boys can't shoot, they can't rebound, they can't even line up properly for a free throw." She ran her finger down the row of scribbles in her notebook. "They do seem to know which players are on their own team, which is an improvement over last year. But it's not enough to win games."

Mr. Dobbs shook his head. "It's not enough for Brett McGrew." He pointed at the big orange sign. "Coach, that boy put Stuckey on the map. He broke every record in the history of Kansas basketball and led this town to the state championship three years running. He's out there now, still doing us proud, breaking NBA records in Phoenix, Arizona."

Mr. Dobbs pulled off his John Deere hat and held it over his heart. I thought for a minute he was going to break into a chorus of "America the Beautiful." But he just took a deep breath and ran his hand through his hair.

Mrs. Zimmer wasn't quite as emotional. "In February, we will be going to Lawrence to be on a national television broadcast. I'm told that Brett McGrew himself will announce our team record. I do not want our town's hero telling the entire country that we haven't won a seventh-grade game in three years." She clicked her pen and dropped it into her purse. "We'll allow you to play your opening game against Whipple. The alumni association already bought pop and hot dogs for the concession stand. Afterward, we'll review your program."

"Review our program," Coach snorted. "So if we don't beat Whipple, we're history."

"If you embarrass us in front of Whipple," said Mrs. Zimmer, "you'll give us no other choice. I will not look foolish on national television."

"You won't *be* on national television, Mrs. Zimmer. The team will."

"You know what I mean, Mr. Armstrong. If you beat Whipple, we'll allow you to continue to play. But you will not go to Lawrence with a losing record."

She tucked her notebook under her arm and strode out

of the gym. Mr. Dobbs settled his John Deere hat back on his head and followed. The door clanked shut.

I stared after them. Canceled? *Canceled?* I'd signed up for basketball, risking such untold humiliation that I might actually have to move to another town once the season ended. And I'd allowed myself to be elected team captain, risking such untold physical injury from Coach that I might have to live at the hospital in my new town. And why was I doing this? For one thing, and one thing only: Brett McGrew. I was finally going to meet him. It might be the only opportunity I ever had.

And Mrs. Zimmer was trying to *cancel* that opportunity? Because of some stupid sports column in a newspaper two hundred miles away?

I was still holding the basketball, and I thudded it against the floor. "New strategy?" *Thud.* "New strategy?" *Thud, thud.* "How's *this* for new strategy?"

I leaned back on one foot, like a major-league pitcher in a windup, and hurled the ball at the basket. It hit the rim, bounced over the backboard, and slammed into Brett McGrew's sign. Right between the two *T*s of Brett's first name.

Coach wasn't paying attention. He was still staring at the door. When that ball ricocheted off the sign, I swear it picked up speed. It shot through the air like a line drive and smacked Coach upside the head.

Coach stumbled.

I groaned.

The ball sailed back over the court in a perfect arc. Over the team. Toward the basket.

Swish. Through the net.

Coach righted himself. Rubbed the red blotch on his cheek as he watched the ball drop. "Huh. Three-pointer." He shook his head. "Probably the only one we'll make all year."

He closed his eyes and stood there for a long time, rubbing his eyelids with his thumb and forefinger.

We stood there, too, afraid to move. The guys looked at me. For leadership, I guess. They were clearly looking in the wrong place. I was still waiting for Coach to crunch me like an empty pop can for walloping him with the basketball.

Finally, Coach stopped digging at his eyeballs. He opened his eyes, rubbed his hand down his face, and gave us a good, long stare.

"You're playing scared."

His voice was a thin rasp, so soft we had to lean forward to hear him. Which, somehow, was more frightening than when he growled so loud it bounced off the bleachers.

"What are you all so afraid of?" He narrowed his eyes. "Of making mistakes? Of looking stupid? Because if that's the case, you all look pretty stupid the way you're tiptoeing around the court, scared to pass, scared to shoot, scared to move out of your positions. You'd look less stupid if—if—"

He stopped. Gave us a funny look. Then he shook his head. Waved a hand toward the locker room.

"Go. Shower. Dress. Do whatever it is seventh graders do at night. We're done."

He tucked the clipboard under his arm and stalked across the court to the lobby door. We stared after him.

And then a voice echoed through the gym. Mine, as it turned out. I have no idea why it chose that moment to assert itself, but there it was: "Coach?"

He stopped, his hand on the door handle. He didn't turn around. "Yeah."

"Well, practice isn't over. We've got practically an hour left, and I really think we need as much court time as we can get. You don't want us to just stop, do you?"

"Stop?" Coach shook his head. Still didn't turn around. "Son, you never started."

He pulled the door open and disappeared into the lobby.

Fifteen

The other guys headed for the showers. I headed toward the supply closet. Turns out cleanliness was a bigger part of this captain business than courage after all. I reached for the mop.

Then stopped. Turned around.

And started thinking.

Here was the thing: Mrs. Zimmer wasn't kidding. We're talking about a woman with zero sense of humor here. When she said we had to beat Whipple or we were finished, she meant it.

But here was the other thing: We couldn't beat Whipple. I didn't know what kind of team they had, but I definitely knew what kind we had.

I hadn't figured on that being a problem. I figured all I had to do was go to practice, try to stay out of the way, and, come February, meet Brett McGrew. That's the deal I signed up for. If I'd known our klutzy bunch had to actually win games, I'd have given this project a whole lot more thought.

I stood there a minute, squinting at the steam that had fogged out of the showers. The guys were still slopping around barefoot, banging locker doors, and slapping their towels onto the floor. I dragged my backpack out of my locker and lugged it to a bench in the far corner. I pulled out my notebook and a freshly sharpened pencil, settled back against the mildew-ridden concrete, and opened my notebook to a fresh page. I wrote *Step Four of The Plan* at the top.

Because Mrs. Zimmer was right. We needed a strategy. There probably wasn't enough strategy in the world to turn this team around. To transform us into actual basketball players. But so far all I'd managed to do was beat my coach senseless with a basketball. Anything I came up with next was bound to be better than that. I drummed my pencil against the page and focused on strategy.

First off, we needed to play to our strengths and minimize our weaknesses. Of course, if we minimized *all* our weaknesses, we wouldn't be playing at all. It would probably be best to concentrate on strengths.

I scribbled down each player's name, then I started listing any known basketball strengths under each one.

First player: Manning Reece. Manning was one of our tallest guys. In fact, he was our only tall guy. He wasn't quick. He couldn't dribble. He got called for traveling almost every time he touched the ball, because he just couldn't get the hang of pivoting. But if he was standing right under the basket and didn't have anybody in his face, he could put it in. Not always. Maybe 50 percent of the time.

If he had somebody guarding him, he'd get so nervous he'd fire the ball right over the backboard. Still, if he was by himself, facing no pressure, he could score some points. That was a strength. We could do something with that. And as tall as he was, if we could get him to actually jump instead of standing there flat-footed like a tree trunk, he might even pull down a couple of rebounds.

I drew a little star by Manning's name.

Second player: Eddie Poggemeyer. Eddie was quick. Fearless. You could count on Eddie to go for the steal or the loose ball or the rebound. You could count on him to relentlessly dog the guy he was defending.

Unfortunately, you could also count on him to foul out in two minutes flat. He wasn't real careful about how he reached in for that steal or loose ball or rebound. He was also a little fuzzy on some of the finer points of the game, like, for instance, how sacking the quarterback is a big achievement in football, but it tends to get you thrown out of basketball games. Plus, he was a complete and total ball hog.

Still, if we could get Eddie to make moves on the perimeter and draw all the defenders away from the basket, then convince him to lob a high pass to Manning (who'd be set up in the low post all by himself, because seriously, who'd be guarding a guy with no obvious basketball skills?), Manning could put it in. We could sneak in a few points that way. At least till the other team caught on.

I put two stars by Eddie's name and another one beside Manning. And made a little note: *Make sure Manning knows he can't just stand in the paint till Eddie throws the pass.* We were going to be making enough mistakes through sheer athletic incompetence. We didn't need to add a three-second violation every time we got the ball.

Next player: Duncan Webber. Short. Slow. No game to speak of. Surprisingly, though, Duncan was our most consistent free-throw shooter. If we could get him to the line, he might actually score some points. Which meant, of course, that he'd have to take a lot of shots in order to *get* to the line. Not something we'd encourage under ordinary circumstances, since Duncan's maybe a worse field-goal shooter than I am.

But what if Duncan was allowed to shoot only at certain times? Say he's surrounded by defenders, guys coming at him from all sides, arms everywhere. Duncan could go ahead and shoot, no matter how little chance he had of actually making the bucket. A foul would almost be guaranteed. He'd get a couple of free throws. And Stuckey would get a point or two.

I put a star by Duncan's name.

Next up: Bragger. I thumped my eraser against the page, trying to think of something Bragger did on the court that could be classified as a strength.

"Hey." A wadded sweat sock skidded across the page. "The reason they call it homework is because you're supposed to do it at home."

I looked up, startled. Except for Bragger and me and about fifty soggy gym towels, the locker room was empty. I'd been so focused on strategy, I hadn't even noticed the other guys had left.

Bragger ambled over to pick up his sock. "Think maybe you could wash the stink off your body and get dressed so we can go home?"

I slid my notebook and pencil into my backpack and headed for the showers.

When Bragger and I tromped into the kitchen, Grandma was going through the mail. She didn't look up. Just handed me another newspaper clipping. This one was a lot smaller. And folded only once.

"Cousin Mildred?" I said.

Grandma nodded. "Lucille Zimmer's letter to the editor made the paper."

"Mrs. Zimmer? Wow." Bragger dumped his backpack by the door. "Stuckey's gotten more press this week than it has in all the years since Brett McGrew graduated."

I dropped my backpack, too, and unfolded the clipping. Bragger crowded in behind me so he could read over my shoulder.

Mrs. Zimmer started off exactly the way she said she would: demanding a full apology. Her rage crackled right off the page. I could imagine her scrawling that letter in her big black notebook, her stern school-board face pinched into a grim pucker.

And even though she'd threatened to cancel seventh-grade basketball, I was in full agreement with her, thinking, *Go, Mrs. Zimmer.*

Till I got to the end of the letter:

Furthermore, although your reporter stated that the Stuckey team will *watch* the University of Kansas retire Brett McGrew's jersey, I assure you, we will not be there merely to watch. We have been invited to *participate*. Our boys will take part in a scrimmage with Brett McGrew at halftime. The seventh-grade Stuckey Prairie Dogs will be playing basketball on the court at Allen Fieldhouse.

"Scrimmage?" I stared at the clipping. "*Scrimmage? We have to scrimmage?*"

"Cool," said Bragger.

"Cool?" I looked at him. "Do you have any idea what this means? It means we have to play basketball. In the fieldhouse. With fans and reporters and the Stuckey school board watching. With TV cameras recording our every pathetic move. What part of that could possibly be cool?" I scanned Mrs. Zimmer's letter. It had to be a mistake. "Why didn't Coach ever mention this? Why wasn't it on the permission slip? It should've been on the permission slip. Everything is supposed to be right there, in writing, on the permission slip. I'm sure it's a school regulation."

Bragger shrugged, obviously not comprehending the seriousness of violating school regulations. "Maybe it was supposed to be a surprise."

"A surprise?"

"And you know," said Bragger, "I don't mean to burst Mrs. Zimmer's bubble, but that sports column guy was kinda right. Except for Brett McGrew and that other player with all those steals, Stuckey hasn't made a dent in the game of basketball. I hate to say it, but without Brett McGrew, Stuckey really *would* be a big, smelly armpit."

"Exactly!" I said, trying to steer the conversation back on track. "Which everyone will see for themselves when the seventh-grade team—of which I am a member—humiliates itself on national television during this *scrimmage*."

"I think you're getting yourself all worked up over nothing, Kirby." Grandma shuffled the mail into a pile and set it on the counter. "I imagine it'll just be a short little exhibition thing. Nobody's going to be paying much attention to you boys, anyway. They'll be too busy watching Brett McGrew."

"Yeah." Bragger's eyes locked onto mine. "Remember him? Brett McGrew? The whole reason we're going? Don't think of it as a scrimmage, Kirby. Think of it as an opportunity to get closer to Brett McGrew."

Oh, yeah, it was an opportunity, all right. An opportunity to show Brett McGrew once and for all I had no business being his son.

Sixteen

Maybe it was Mrs. Zimmer. Maybe it was the bump on the head. Whatever it was, Coach started acting strange, even for Coach.

I really didn't have time to think about Coach. Not at first. I was too busy thinking about the scrimmage. I thought about it all weekend, and by Monday morning, I'd come up with an amazingly brilliant Step Five: Take a Dive.

Literally.

During practice, sometime before we went to Lawrence, I'd make a maniac dive to keep the ball in bounds, or a wild leap to bring down a rebound, or an insane lunge for a steal, and *presto*: a sprained ankle, a pulled hamstring, a mangled tendon. That's all it would take to keep me on the bench during the KU scrimmage. I'd get to meet Brett McGrew, but I wouldn't frighten him by actually trying to play basketball.

It was the perfect plan. I couldn't fail. Falling down was maybe my best talent. All I had to do was take that talent to the next level. Fall down harder, faster, and with a little more rotation.

The injury itself was pretty ingenious, but here was the brilliant part: With all that adhesive tape plus an Ace bandage and maybe an ice pack or two wrapped around the damaged body part, I'd look athletic. More athletic than I'd ever looked in my life. Shoot, wearing that much medical gear, I'd look positively All-American.

And to top it all off, when we got to the fieldhouse, I'd make a big show of trying to get into the game. But of course, my injury would be too serious to allow me any playing time, so I'd grimace in pain and hobble back to the bench. Acting all disappointed, of course. Any uncoordination on my part (and there *would* be uncoordination— we're talking about me, after all) would be blamed on the injury, not on my own personal lack of motor skills.

Amazing how much a sprained ankle could cheer me up. I actually started to *feel* All-American. Not in the athletic sense, of course. I wasn't completely delusional. But in the figuring-things-out sense. The sense that no matter what Coach or Mrs. Zimmer or anybody else threw at me, I'd figure out how to deal with it.

I was feeling so All-American, in fact, that I'd actually talked myself into showing Coach my list of team strengths and possible plays. It was good strategy. And it could work. It could totally work.

Of course, it could totally fail, too. We weren't dealing with a real talent pool here.

But if we picked out the things we were good at and concentrated on them, we might just win some games. If nothing else, we'd confuse the other team for a while. They'd probably never seen anybody do the things we were good at. Not on purpose, anyway.

Monday after school, armed with my list and pumped up with temporary courage, I trotted into practice with Bragger. We found all the windows in the gym taped over with black bulletin-board paper. Which all by itself should've tipped us off that something was up. Something we didn't want any part of.

And, just in case we didn't catch on right away, Coach was waiting by the locker room door. Behind a big stack of boxes. Bright red with a big swirl and the words STEALTH SPORTSWEAR in gold. The blotch on the side of his face had turned into an angry purple bruise.

Final clue: when Coach stepped out from behind the boxes, he was naked.

Okay, not *naked* naked. But close enough. Closer than I ever wanted to see. He stood there, right in the middle of the gym, wearing nothing but his undershorts and whistle. Hands on his hips. Hairy chest puffed up. Knobby chicken legs poking out beneath his boxers.

By this time, the other guys had all traipsed into the gym. And stopped cold. We stood in a startled huddle, all twelve of us, trying not to stare at Coach. It was like a train wreck—so horrible you didn't want to look, and at the same time, so horrible you couldn't tear your eyes away.

"Everybody at the beauty parlor was laying bets on what Coach would do next," Duncan whispered. "Boy, are *they* all going to lose."

Coach flipped his clipboard under his arm and paced over to stand directly in front of us.

"Listen up," he barked. "This"—he pointed at his bare stomach—"is highly advanced technology."

We glanced at each other out of the corners of our eyes.

Coach pulled out an official-looking document with a gold seal on the cover. "You're looking at a Stealth Warm-up Suit, gentlemen. Developed by the Marine Corps." He tapped the document. "Completely undetectable by radar."

We stared at him.

"Lightweight. Aerodynamic." Coach flexed his shoulders. "Fits like your own skin." He flipped the document open and ran his finger down the page. "Forty-two percent less wind resistance." He looked up at us. "Thirty-eight percent less gravity."

"Less gravity?" Eddie whispered. "You can't get less gravity. Unless you go to the moon."

Russell shook his head. "I think that's where Coach is."

"And tough." Coach punched himself in the chest. "Like wearing full-body armor." He slapped the document shut and looked at us for a long moment. "This technology is powerful, gentlemen. In the wrong hands, frankly, it could be dangerous. Which is why the Defense Department included a built-in fail-safe. If I couldn't handle this technology, you wouldn't be able to see this."

He held out his arms and turned slowly, so we could get a good look. Turns out his back was as hairy as his front. Information I truly didn't need.

"Because for those who aren't winners, for those who don't have what it takes to control the technology, the uniforms are"—Coach stopped turning and squinted from player to player—"invisible."

We stood there, mouths open.

"Did he say what I think he said?" Bragger hissed.

Eddie nodded. "He must be using a Stealth Brain."

Coach paced over to the stack of boxes. "Stealth technology enhances all your physical skills. Helps you run faster. Jump higher. Play longer." He thumped the top box. "Stealth technology is going to help us beat Whipple." He held the box out to Duncan, who had no choice but to take it. "These are Stealth Uniforms, gentlemen." He handed a box to Manning. "It takes time to get used to the new speed and agility, to get the uniforms functioning fully with your body's natural current, so starting today, we'll wear them at every practice."

We froze. *Every. Practice.*

As Coach passed out the boxes, he grunted a few things about the science behind the uniforms. When he reached the bottom of the stack, he gave us a long, hard look. "Remember. " He narrowed his eyes. A vein pulsed in the purple bruise. "Only true winners have what it takes to control Stealth power. So if you got a problem with your uniform, if you can't handle it, you got no business on my team. Do I make myself clear?"

We stood there, all twelve of us, holding our suspiciously lightweight boxes, and nodded like bobbleheads.

"Another thing." Coach planted his fists on his hips. "These uniforms are our secret weapon. We don't want

Whipple finding out about them. Which is why the windows are taped over. What we do in the gym, stays in the gym. Our plays, drills, lineups, uniforms—all strictly classified information. Got it?"

The bobbleheads bobbled.

"Good. Now suit up. Let's see how they fit."

Seventeen

Well, they fit like skin, just like Coach promised.

We milled around the locker room in our underwear, shaking our heads, empty boxes scattered on the floor around us. Of course, they'd been empty before we ever opened them.

I stared at the boxes. I couldn't believe it. I'd spent all this time doing everything I could to get the team to Lawrence, and the whole world, including my coach, was working against me. Every time I got it figured out, every time I came up with a new strategy, something worse happened. All weekend, while I worked out Step Five, I kept telling myself that if we could get past this—past the school board, past a losing season, past the KU scrimmage—we were home free. Because nothing could be worse than me playing basketball in front of my father.

Ha.

I felt like hitting something. Of course, last time I felt that way, I'd ended up smacking Coach into a stupor with a basketball.

"I don't get it." Duncan sat huddled at the end of a bench, clutching a red box lid over his bare belly, trying his best not to be naked. "Coach is loud. And tough. And sometimes he's just plain mean. But he's not stupid. Why would he give us invisible jerseys?"

Eddie rolled his eyes. "They're not invisible, Duncan. They don't exist." He ripped the lid from Duncan's hands and waved it above his head. "Coach handed you a box of air."

"I know that." Duncan snatched his lid back. "I'm not stupid, either. I just don't know what else to call"—he waved the lid at his pasty white goose-bumpy self—"this."

We all looked at Duncan's nakedness. I don't think any of us knew what to call it.

"Here's what I don't get," said Russell. "Does Coach really believe all that stuff he told us? Or is this some kind of trick? I mean, how dumb does he think we are?"

"Yeah." Eddie nodded. "What was that business about electrical impulses?"

"According to Coach," said Manning, "if you've got the right charge, you're okay. If you don't—"

"—you're naked," said Russell.

Eddie shook his head. "Right. Like we're really supposed to believe we've got electricity zapping around inside us."

"Actually," I said, "we do."

The guys all turned to stare at me.

I swallowed. "Really. We do. You know brain waves? They're electrical currents that flow through our brain cells all the time."

Eddie narrowed his eyes. "So . . . what? You're saying all that junk Coach told us is true?"

"No. No way." I held up my hands. "I'm just saying that, you know, we do have inner electrical currents. It's possible that someday—maybe—in the future, somebody could harness their power. In some way. But not for this. Not for basketball uniforms."

"Yeah," said Bragger. "And even if that electrical impulse stuff was true, you've still got that business about antigravity and invisibility. Which we all know is demented." He punched my arm, obviously trying to ride to my rescue. "Right, Kirb?"

"Well . . . ," I said.

Eddie narrowed his eyes again. "Well what?"

"Well." I swallowed. "Some people have theories. It's all pretty complicated, involving electromagnetic fields, refracted light rays, and centrifugal force, but someday—maybe—in the future—"

"Man." Eddie shook his head. "You must spend all your free time memorizing the Science Channel or something."

"Well, I don't care what might be possible someday. Or on what planet." Russell pointed at his red-and-white striped briefs. "I can't go out there like this."

"You? How do you think *I* feel?" Manning snapped his Spiderman undershorts. "My grandma gave me ten pairs of these for my birthday. I got nothing but superheroes in my underwear drawer."

I looked down at my gray boxer briefs. They weren't as humiliating as Spidey-pants, but I sure didn't want to parade them around the gym. Still—

I took a deep breath. "We have to."

The guys stared at me.

"What?"

"You heard Coach," I said. "If we don't wear his uniforms, we're off the team."

Eddie snorted. "News flash, Nickel. Once Mrs. Zimmer gets wind of this, there won't *be* a team."

"No kidding," said Russell. "If she thought losing was embarrassing, wait till she finds out Coach wants us to lose in our underwear."

"Then she can't find out." I looked at them. "Coach said it himself: 'What we do in the gym, stays in the gym.' And Coach isn't talking. So as long as *we* don't talk, nobody'll know."

"So what are you saying?" Duncan hugged the lid close to his belly. "You're saying we just march out there in our underwear and act like it's normal?"

The guys looked at me.

"Yeah." Bragger nodded. "That's exactly what he's saying. The windows in the gym are all taped over, so it's not really any different than being in the locker room. We see each other's underwear in here every day. Now we'll see them a little bit more. That's all." The jack-o'-lantern grin spread across his face. "Besides, none of you guys has to go first. Kirby's our team captain. He'll lead the way."

Gee, thanks, Bragger.

"And if Kirby can strut out there wearing next to nothing . . ." Bragger looked directly at Eddie.

Who narrowed his eyes. "Hey, I can do it, too." He shot a glance at me. No way Eddie was going to let anybody else, especially not a scrawny wimp like Kirby Nickel, look more fearless than he did.

"Good." Bragger turned to the other guys. "Russell?"

Russell glared at him. "If they can take it, I can take it."

"Manning?"

Manning swallowed. And nodded.

One by one, all the guys agreed. Reluctantly. But they agreed. Nobody wanted to be the sissy who couldn't take it.

"Wait a minute," said Duncan. "Let's say we practice in our underwear. We're still forgetting one thing: Someday practice is going to end, and we'll have to play a real game. Against another team. With our parents and the whole rest of the school and Mrs. Zimmer watching. What then? Huh?"

Yeah. What then?

Eighteen

Grandma says whatever doesn't kill us makes us stronger. Which told me that when this whole thing was over, I'd either be dead or Arnold Schwarzenegger. Either one sounded better than nearly naked captain of a seventh-grade basketball team.

But there we were: twelve guys and their coach, standing in a middle school gymnasium, trying not to stare at each other's underwear. Wind rattled the papered-over windows behind us, sending a goose-bumpy shiver through my whole body.

Coach watched us for a long moment. Trying to figure out, I guess, whether we were having any trouble with our new uniforms. Whether he'd have to cut anybody from the team.

But we weren't admitting anything. We hunkered down behind each other, our hands and arms wrapped around as much of our bare selves as we could cover. But we didn't say a word.

Finally, Coach tucked his clipboard under his hairy armpit. "All right, we've wasted enough practice time. Let's get warmed up. And I want to see some hustle."

Oh, we hustled, all right. You've never seen how low the game of basketball can sink till you've seen a bunch of no-talent seventh graders hustling through a full-court press in their underpants. And one of those seventh graders—me—diving for every loose ball like a bird dog on steroids.

And, sadly, coming through it with all his body parts intact.

Because naked or not, I had an ankle to twist and a limited amount of time to twist it in. Unfortunately, it turns out I have frighteningly strong ankles. My legs are knobby and scrawny and look like they might snap in two just from trying to hold up my Jammers, but I have the sturdiest ankles in recorded history. I couldn't get one of those suckers to twist no matter how funny I came down on it or how hard I landed. Or how many other guys landed on top of me.

Coach watched me all through practice, his face knotted into a frown. Every time I peeled myself off the floor, I'd look up, and there'd be Coach. Watching. I felt like a bug in a jar. A hopelessly uncoordinated bug. With ankles of steel.

But there was a reason I noticed him watching me. I was watching him, too. Secretly. Between crashing to the floor and heaving myself back up. Because Russell had made a good point. Did Coach really believe this Stealth Uniform business? Did he seriously think the uniforms existed? That they'd make us run faster and jump higher? And turn invisible if we didn't?

Or was he messing with our heads?

I studied Coach as he pressed us through an inbounding

drill. Was he using some kind of sports psychology on us? Some bizarro kind of sports psychology? I'd heard of coaches making their team practice without a ball. But without clothes?

We ran through the drill a few more times, then finished with some free throws. As we filed toward the locker room, coach blew out a big breath, shook his head, and strode from the gym.

The other guys showered and dressed. I hauled my backpack to the bench in the far corner. The bench I was starting to think of as my office. I pulled out my notebook, opened it to a fresh page, and drew a line down the middle to make two columns. At the top of the first column, I printed: *Coach Believes They Exist*. Under it, I wrote down the evidence I'd gathered so far:

1. Coach keeps observing us—me, especially. Maybe he's trying to figure out who he has to cut from the team. Maybe he's decided I'm first.

2. Coach didn't mention the loser factor. Not once, even though we didn't run faster, jump higher, or demonstrate any of the new skills Stealth technology is supposed to give us. Even though we were obviously naked. Maybe he's giving our electrical currents time to kick in.

I thumped the eraser against my bottom lip and studied the list. Then I printed *Coach Is Psyching Us Out* at the top of the second column. I thought about it for a moment, then scribbled down all the evidence I'd gathered in that category:

1. Coach keeps observing us—me, especially. Maybe he's trying to figure out if his psychology experiment is working. Maybe I'm his chief guinea pig.

2. He didn't mentioned the loser factor. Not once, even though we didn't run faster or jump higher. Even though we were all obviously naked. Maybe he's giving his psychology experiment time to kick in.

I looked at the page. So far it didn't add up to much. Coach was acting funny, yeah. But he hadn't done anything that definitely pointed one way or the other. Anything that proved he'd either lost his mind or was messing with ours. I closed my notebook and slipped it back into my backpack. I'd have to keep watching him.

Nineteen

Practice the next day started out pretty much the same: Coach watched the team, I secretly watched Coach, the other guys tiptoed around, all hunched over, trying to make their naked bodies as small as possible while I did my best to pop one of my bones from its socket.

Coach really watched during a rebound drill in which I slashed to the basket at approximately 110 miles per hour and fired a layup. Which didn't go in, of course. In my defense, since this was a rebounding drill, it wasn't supposed to go in, which meant that, for the first time in my life, my substandard shooting ability really came in handy.

But I wasn't finished. I spun across the paint, in front of Duncan, who was supposed to be doing the rebounding, pulled down my own offensive board, and vaulted toward the basket to lay the ball in.

And, unfortunately, landed square on both feet. No torn muscles. No popping joints. No excruciating pain. The ball even went through the hoop.

I was so disappointed.

Coach wasn't. He blew his whistle. "Looks like Nickel's been taking his vitamins." He grunted, Coach's version of a compliment. "He's obviously got this Stealth technology down pat. You other guys need to watch and learn."

Oh, brother. That was the wrong thing to say in front of Eddie. We were probably the most athletically challenged class to ever pass through the Stuckey unified school system, but even a klutzy bunch like ours has to have a best athlete, a kid who's clearly less uncoordinated than the others. For us, that kid was Eddie Poggemeyer.

And Eddie wasn't about to learn anything sports related from an all-elbows math geek like Kirby Nickel. He wasn't about to let Kirby Nickel—or anybody else, for that matter—master Stealth technology before he did. He certainly wasn't going to stand by and do nothing while Coach informed an entire team of basketball players that Kirby Nickel could do something in a gymnasium better than Eddie himself could.

Personally, I didn't care who was the best athlete. I'd figured out a long time ago it would never be me, which was the whole reason I was trying to inflict bodily injury on myself in the first place. I didn't want to impress anybody. I just wanted to strain a major muscle group.

But to Eddie's mind, Coach had issued a personal challenge.

I could see that mind working. Could see Eddie eyeballing me. Then eyeballing his own bare skin. Could practically see the gears cranking in his head as he tried to figure out which one was worse.

Finally he stepped out from behind Russell, stood up straight and tall in his ratty green jockey shorts, and said, "Give me the ball."

I passed the basketball. Eddie caught it in one hand, dribbled between his legs, then stormed the basket. He banged the ball off the backboard, caught it at the top of his leap, and fired it back up before his feet touched the ground. The ball dropped through the hoop.

Eddie turned and glared at me. "Offensive rebound and two points. Would've been an alley-oop if I was a little taller. Unassisted." He fired the ball into my chest.

And from that moment on, basketball practice officially became a competition.

I leaped for a rebound. Eddie leaped higher. I slashed for the basket. Eddie slashed harder. I dove for a loose ball. Eddie hurtled over me, leaped toward the bleachers, and slapped the ball back in bounds before crashing to the floor. Whatever I did, Eddie did, too, only bigger, stronger, faster.

Well. Bragger wasn't going to let two other guys steal all the glory. Bragger wasn't what you'd call athletically gifted, but lack of ability had never stopped him before.

And nakedness wasn't going to stop him now.

He decided three-point land was his. He fired shot after shot from beyond the arc. Some of them actually went in. The ones that didn't? No problem. Because as soon as Bragger shot, he stormed the basket to bang down the rebound.

Russell watched. Russell, who, despite a miserable scoring percentage, liked to think of himself as king of the three-point bucket. He watched Bragger shoot. And rebound. And shoot again.

Finally he peeled his arms from around his body, glanced down at his red-and-white striped briefs, and marched out to center court.

He bagged a couple of three pointers and pulled down a few boards of his own. And blocked a couple of Manning's shots under the basket, which woke Manning up and taught him the value of the pump fake.

One by one, each player stopped worrying about his underwear and started worrying about running faster and jumping higher. By the end of practice, the whole team seemed to be making a run for Best Athlete—lunging for steals, exploding toward the basket, guarding their man like he was an escaped convict.

Duncan even got in on the action. He actually started jogging down the court during the scrimmage instead of trudging along at his usual out-of-breath pace. He was still moving slowly compared to your average kid, but for Duncan, it was warp speed.

When practice was over, we filed into the locker room, sweaty and out of breath. Coach shook his head. "Stealth Uniforms are paying off sooner than I thought."

Twenty

I pulled my notebook from my backpack and opened it to the right page. I set it on the chipped tabletop, smoothed my hand across the paper, and scribbled:

> 3. Coach says Stealth Uniforms are pay-
> ing off sooner than he thought.

I sighed. One more for the *Coach Believes They Exist* column. I thumped my pencil eraser on the sad excuse for a lunch table we called The Hulk, trying to dredge up more evidence for our side.

Bragger shoveled a forkful of toxic waste—chicken and noodles this time—into his mouth. "Good guys losing?"

"Not yet." I studied my list. "I haven't been able to collect enough data to support either theory. But it isn't looking good. Coach sure *acts* like he believes in Stealth technology."

I sighed again. Closed the notebook, tucked my pencil inside, and slid it into my backpack.

And looked up just in time to see Eddie headed our way, lunch tray in hand. Russell and Manning followed close behind, like ducklings trailing their mother duck.

Eddie scootched his way around to the other side of

The Hulk. He set his tray down across from me and slid into the chair. The ducklings sat down beside him.

Bragger and I looked at each other.

"Hey, Eddie," said Bragger. "Glad you could join us."

"Uh-huh." Eddie shot a sideways glance at Russell. "We thought we should talk. You know, like a team meeting."

I shrugged. "Okay."

I noticed Duncan making his way across the lunch-room. He reached The Hulk. Saw Eddie and Russell sitting there. And stopped short.

Eddie saw him, too. "Grab a seat," he said. "This involves you."

Duncan blinked. Glanced behind him to see who Eddie was talking to. Didn't find anybody and turned back around. "Are you sure?"

"It's okay, Duncan." Bragger motioned his head toward the seat next to him. "Sit down."

Duncan nodded and slid into his seat, taking great care not to bump the napkin wad.

Eddie took a bite of chicken and noodles. He chewed and swallowed. Gave me a squinty-eyed look. "I don't like wearing my underwear in public."

"Me, neither," said Russell.

"Yeah," said Manning.

I cut a look at Bragger. Who shrugged.

"Nobody thinks you do," I said.

Eddie glanced from Duncan to Bragger to me. "Because yesterday in practice, when I was, you know, shooting and stuff? In my underwear? I didn't enjoy it. I just didn't want Coach getting mad at me. Thinking I couldn't play. That's all."

"That's all," said Russell.

"Yeah," said Manning.

Eddie slurped up another mouthful of noodles. " 'Cause here's the thing." He chewed while he thought about it. "If Coach really believes these stupid uniforms exist, then he really believes they'll make us play better. So if we don't play better, he's going to get suspicious. He's going to think we don't have what it takes."

"To wear the uniforms," said Russell.

"Yeah," said Manning.

Bragger nodded. "You've got a point."

"So all I'm saying is, I'm going to keep playing hard. In my underwear. But that doesn't mean I like it." Eddie sucked up the last of his milk, then crushed the carton. "That's all I'm saying." He scooted his chair back and stood up. Glanced around the table. "So we're cool, right?"

"Yeah," I said. "We're cool. I mean, who likes playing in their underwear?"

Eddie nodded, then carried his tray over to the dump bin. The ducklings waddled along in his wake. Bragger rolled his eyes, picked up his tray, and followed them.

"I do."

Duncan's voice was soft.

I looked at him. "You do what?"

He swallowed. "Like playing in my underwear. You

111

asked who liked it, and, well, I do." He twirled his fork in his noodles. "At first it was weird, but once we got going, I—I didn't mind. I mean, you know, not in a twisted way." He sneaked a glance at me. "But the way it made us all kind of the same? That's what I liked." His already slumpy shoulders slumped even lower. "I guess I just get tired of being the dorkiest kid in the gym."

I looked at him. Sure, he leaned toward the dork side. But I always thought *I* was the dorkiest.

Duncan stabbed his noodles. "No matter where I go or what I do, you can count on me to look stupider than anyone else. But yesterday, when we were all in our underwear, *everybody* looked stupid. Just as stupid as me. It's almost like I fit in." He shrugged. "As well as I'm ever going to, anyway." He glanced up. Frowned. "You won't tell anybody, will you? I mean, it's not like a team captain duty or something, is it? To tell about stuff like this?"

I shook my head. "Don't worry, Duncan. Your secret's safe."

Duncan nodded. "Okay. Good." He mustered a weak smile. "Thanks, Kirby."

He picked up his tray and scuffled off to the dump bin.

I watched him. And thought, well *yeah,* his secret's safe. I couldn't possibly tell anybody. Because then I'd have to tell them Duncan was right. That I totally understood how he felt.

Twenty-one

Eddie wasn't kidding. He said he was going to play hard, no matter what he had to wear or not wear, and he meant it. He was a maniac at practice. Dribbling. Shooting. Rebounding. Not passing, of course. He was a ball hog to begin with, plus how could he show Coach what Stealth technology was doing for him if he didn't have the ball? But stealing? Oh, yeah. He was a klepto in gym shoes.

The whole team acted like they'd overdosed on sports drinks. They didn't show any improvement in skill. Or teamwork. But they really latched onto that running-faster, jumping-higher business. I'd never seen so many guys running in so many directions before. Into the bleachers. Into the wrestling mats. Into each other. It was a miracle, really, that nobody got hurt.

But nobody did. Not even the one guy who was trying to. My ankles came through, strong as ever. Maybe even stronger. All that jumping around seemed to build up my ankle muscles.

Coach watched with a stunned look on his face. Rubbed a hand over his eyes. "I've created a monster," he mumbled. "Twelve of them."

I thought about that. About what it could mean.

Seemed to me like something a guy would say about a science project that had gone horribly wrong. So that's where I put it, in the science experiment column. After practice, while the other guys showered and changed, I scuffed across the damp concrete to the bench in the corner and pulled out my notebook. Under column two, *Coach Is Psyching Us Out*, I wrote:

> 3. Coach says he's created a monster. Like Dr. Frankenstein.

I studied the two columns. Tied at three apiece. I thumped my pencil against the page. There had to be something more. Something I'd overlooked. I thought back to everything that had happened since Coach passed out those empty boxes. And remembered what Duncan said in the locker room.

In Column #2 I scribbled:

> 4. Coach might be mean, but he isn't stupid.

That made it four to three. I shut my notebook. And decided it was time to implement Step Six of The Plan. Or was it Step Seven? I'd lost count.

I waited till most of the guys had changed and gone home, then knocked on Coach's door. I heard a grunt, which could've been either "Come in" or "Get lost." With

Coach, it was hard to tell. I glanced back at Bragger, the only guy left in the locker room. He nodded and gave me a thumbs-up.

I took a deep breath, turned the knob, and poked my head inside. My spiral notebook rattled in my hand.

"Uh, Coach?"

He'd already showered and changed. Attempting to give the guy coaching tips was scary enough. I sure didn't need to stare at his hairy chest muscles while I did it. But Coach was back in his regular clothes, hunched over his desk, studying a newspaper. A newspaper that looked oddly familiar.

He ran a hand over his chin. "You know who this player is, Nickel?" he said without looking up.

I squinted at the paper upside down. It was the Kansas City *Star*. The sports page. The one with the Armpit column.

I frowned. "You mean Brett McGrew?"

Coach snorted. "Good guess. Usually somebody says 'player,' you can pretty much bet they mean Brett McGrew. But I'm talking about this other guy." He thumped his finger on the paper. "This guy with all the steals. You know his name?"

I shook my head. "No, sir."

"Didn't think so. Can't find anybody who does." He leaned forward, fists folded together, elbows on the paper. "So. What can I do for you, Nickel?"

I was still standing in the doorway, one shoulder in his

office, the other still in the locker room, in case I found it necessary to back out in a hurry.

"Well." I pulled my notebook around to the office side of the doorway. "I know I'm not the coach. I'm just a player. But I'm the team captain, and as such, I feel it's, well, my duty to be on the lookout for ways to improve our play, to help us, you know, win. So I've written down a few things, a few plays that might work—or maybe they won't, maybe you won't like them, maybe they're really bad ideas, and that's okay because we don't have to use them—but I just thought I should at least write these down, you know, in case—"

"Just show me what you got, Nickel."

"Yes, sir."

With shaky hands, I tore the play pages loose, scuttled into the office, and set them on the desk in front of Coach.

And waited for him to wad them into a ball. And then wad me up, too. And stuff us both into his trash can.

He picked up the first page, scanned it, scanned the second page, then went back to the first page and read more carefully.

"Not bad, Nickel. Pull the defenders off Reece, try to keep Poggemeyer out of foul trouble, get Webber to the line." He squinted at the sheet for a long moment. Then he looked up. "Mind if I keep this?"

I shook my head.

"Good. I'll study it." He glanced back at the first page. "This Reece play. You know, this might work. We ran a play something like this one time. The other team was so worried about stopping McGrew that they pretty much forgot about—"

"McGrew?" I stared at Coach. "*Brett* McGrew?"

"You know another McGrew?"

"You played with him? You played a basketball game with Brett McGrew?"

Coach narrowed his eyes. Studied me while he ran his tongue over his teeth. "Yeah. I played a basketball game with Brett McGrew."

"Wow." I shook my head in wonder. "So you knew him. You actually met him." I looked up. "What was he like?"

"What was he like?" Coach snorted. "Tall guy with a wicked slash to the basket. What'd you think he was like?"

"What I meant was—" I stopped. I couldn't tell Coach what I meant. "I mean, not *me* exactly. I don't personally want to know. But the other guys, what they've been, you know, talking about in the locker room, is what he's like as a person. You know, is he friendly? To, say, strangers? Does he have any—"

Any what? Kids? Sons? Offspring he may or may not know about?

"—pets?"

"Pets?" Coach leaned back in his chair. "I got a basketball team going to Lawrence to meet a major NBA star, to scrimmage with him, maybe pick up a pointer or two, and what they're wondering is, does he have *pets*?"

"Well, maybe not pets. That wasn't a good example. I just want—I mean, the *team* just wants to know what to expect. If he'll be nice to them. And as team captain, I feel it's my duty to help out. In this area. Of, you know, whether he's nice. Or not."

"Uh-huh." Coach studied me. He shook his head, then folded up the newspaper in front of him. "Tell your teammates to relax. Brett McGrew's a good guy. Fearless. Relentless. Got ice water running through his veins during a game. But he's a decent person." He dropped the paper into the wastebasket by his desk. "Hard guy to hate."

Twenty-two

Okay. Brett McGrew was a hard guy to hate. I wrote that down in my notebook, right under *Likes biscuits and gravy.*

Step Six had gone pretty smoothly. A lot better than I'd expected, especially since I'd managed to sneak a Surprise Bonus Step Six-and-a-Half into the action: Ask Coach about Brett McGrew. I closed my notebook and got ready for Step Seven.

Bragger and I had dropped off our film to get developed after the Halloween dance, and now the pictures were ready. So after practice, we pulled the hoods of our coats snug around our ears to ward off the biting November wind and trekked down to the drugstore to pick them up. I'd stowed the necessary equipment in my backpack: a magnifying glass, one of Grandma's photo albums that held recent pictures of me in various poses, and a pocket full of quarters in case we needed to blow up any of the Brett McGrew photos on the drugstore copier.

I paid for the pictures, and we settled down on the wide ledge inside the front windows. I opened Grandma's photo album and set it on the matted brown carpeting between us. The wind whistled against the fogged-up windows at our backs while heat ducts blasted hot air at our feet.

I peeled off my coat and bunched it up behind me to fend off the cold, then pulled the stack of shiny new photos from the packet. The first one was the accidental picture of Coach's back as he gazed into the trophy case, the one I'd snapped when I almost dropped the camera. It was all big and sharp and in focus, thanks to Bragger's dad's super-deluxe auto-crisp zoom lens.

Waste of film. I handed it off to Bragger.

Next photo: a row of gleaming trophies with a picture of Brett McGrew nestled in the middle. Then another photo of another row of gleaming trophies with another picture of Brett McGrew in the middle. Then gleaming medals and another picture of Brett McGrew. Newspaper clippings about Brett McGrew, featuring pictures of Brett McGrew, all in gleaming frames. Team pictures with Brett McGrew featured prominently in the center. And, of course, three photos of the big cutout poster of Brett McGrew.

Nothing I hadn't expected to see.

And nothing that looked like me no matter which angle I tipped the magnifying glass or how much I squinted. I simply could not find any part of my own unimpressive seventh-grade self in all those pictures of Brett McGrew, Future NBA Superstar. I handed the magnifying glass to Bragger, who went over the pictures, too. And came up with nothing.

The front door whooshed open, and the wind scattered the pictures. Bragger and I scrambled to gather them up.

"Hey, look!" Bragger plucked a photo from the floor. "We almost missed it."

"We did?" I ripped the picture from his hands. Stared at it. At the accidental picture I'd taken of Coach. "What are you talking about? This isn't even a picture we tried to take."

"I know. But look. Coach's face is reflected off the glass."

"So?"

"So." Bragger trained the magnifying glass over the photo. "His face is reflected right beside that picture he was staring at. The team picture. See?"

I saw. Varsity team. Brett McGrew's freshman year. Brett McGrew in his number 5 jersey sitting in the middle of the front row. Most freshmen didn't play varsity. But most freshmen weren't Brett McGrew.

And this Brett McGrew didn't look any more like me than the other ones did. "What am I supposed to be looking at?" I said.

"Here at the end. Number twenty-three." Bragger held the magnifying glass over the picture.

I looked. At player number twenty-three. Then, as Bragger moved the magnifying glass, at the reflection on the trophy case.

"It's Coach." I blinked. "Number twenty-three is Coach."

"Sure looks like it."

"Coach played basketball with Brett McGrew."

121

"Sure looks like it."

"No. He did. He told me. Just a little bit ago. Coach said he played basketball with Brett McGrew. I thought he meant maybe they played once in some kind of coaches' clinic or something, and Brett McGrew showed up as a visiting guest of honor or something. I didn't know he meant a real game." I stared at the picture. "A bunch of real games."

Bragger moved the magnifying glass from the team photo to Coach's reflection, then back again. "It sure does explain a lot."

I looked at him. "This is why Coach wants to go to Lawrence. Why he's so desperate to get there."

Bragger studied the picture thoughtfully for a moment. "And why Mrs. Zimmer agreed to let him go. I mean, she wants this retirement ceremony to be perfect." He tapped the picture. "And what could be more perfect than this?"

I nodded. Sometimes he was brilliant. Bragger Barnes, my cousin, brilliant.

"You're right," I said. "Coach and Brett McGrew played together for Stuckey. Coach was there to witness the beginning of Brett McGrew's greatness. Coach was there when Brett McGrew led the team to all those state championships. And now Coach'll bring a Stuckey team to Lawrence to honor Brett McGrew when he gets his jersey retired."

"The sports reporters at the KU game are going to jump all over this," said Bragger. "It's the kind of cheesy heartwarming story they just love. It does kind of choke you up."

"Yeah. It's like—like fate or something."

"Like a TV movie waiting to happen," said Bragger. "Mrs. Zimmer's probably already got somebody all picked out to play her."

"Probably." I thought about it for a minute. "She's not going to be happy if her movie ends with twelve guys and their coach showing up at Allen Fieldhouse in their underpants."

Bragger nodded. "I can't say I'd be real happy with that ending myself."

Twenty-three

The next day at lunch, Bragger and I carried our trays to The Hulk.

And found Eddie, Russell, and Manning already sitting there.

Bragger raised his eyebrows. "Team meeting?"

Eddie shrugged and shook his head. Gnawed on a bite of hot dog. "Just eating lunch."

Bragger and I looked at each other and slid into our chairs.

Duncan shuffled toward us, tray in hand. He motioned his head toward the empty seat next to Eddie. "That's probably saved, huh?"

Eddie glanced at Duncan. "Nope. Sit down."

Duncan stood there for a second, stunned. Then he scurried around the table, giving the napkin wad a wide berth, and settled down next to Eddie.

The next day, we all sat together at The Hulk again. A couple of other players wandered over and joined us. The next day, a couple more. By the end of the week, the whole team was sitting there. Eating. Laughing. Trying to gross each other out by digging wax out of their ears with their carrot sticks. Duncan still looked a little nervous. Like he was afraid somebody'd suddenly realize he was sitting there and tell him to beat it. But he laughed at the ear wax, too.

Bragger glanced around the table. "Weird."

"I know." I shook my head. "Almost makes Stealth Uniforms seem sane."

It was funny. Keeping this secret together like we were, well, it sort of bonded us together. It started in the lunchroom, but pretty soon it spilled over into practice.

There we were, running around in our underwear, with absolutely nothing to hide and no way to hide it anyway, and really, with nobody in the gym who cared what we were wearing. All that was left was basketball. So we played.

During a scrimmage a few days later, Manning passed the ball to Eddie, and Duncan, against all odds, managed to step into the passing lane at just the right moment. He reached for the steal, tripped, and skidded out of bounds with the ball.

Eddie held a hand out to pull him off the floor and—I'm not kidding—said, "Nice try, Webber." And he was sincere. Not being a smart aleck. And then—no kidding—he said, "Hey, next time try not to lunge with your whole body. Move your feet and just reach for the ball with your outside hand. Like this. See? That way, you don't get off balance."

Now, I'd never heard Eddie give anybody sports praise. Or sports advice. Especially not Duncan. And especially not after Duncan had picked off a pass intended for Eddie.

But there he was, showing Duncan how he could steal the ball without taking a header into the bleachers.

And then—I *swear* this is true—he called Duncan "Big D." Yeah, Big D. And not sarcastically, like you'd expect out of Eddie. Sincerely. With respect. Like Duncan was Eddie's buddy or something. A buddy named Big D.

When Duncan heard that, his chest swelled and he stepped up his game a little.

On the next play, Russell pulled down a rebound and thundered up the court, making a fast break for the basket. He was surrounded by defenders, three on one, and instead of trying to make the bucket himself like he normally would, he pump-faked, then kicked the ball out to Bragger, who was wide open at the top of the key. Bragger slipped in behind the defenders and laid in the easy bucket. I almost fell over. I had just witnessed the first assist in the history of our team.

Russell and Bragger banged their fists together, Russell as proud of his pass as Bragger was of his basket.

Coach saw all this, of course, eyes squinted. And his snarling took on a new tone. He still yelled at us every time we breathed, of course. But instead of yelling that we were uncoordinated sissies who couldn't make a basket if the hoop was ten feet wide and three feet off the ground, he started yelling things like, "A little more follow-through and you'll own that shot, Barnes." And, "Pretty good pass fake, Wiles, but don't telegraph with your head." And, when Duncan was lying under the basket, eyes rolled back in their sockets, gasping for oxygen, "Way to take a charge, Webber."

At the end of practice Friday, he gathered us around the blackboard in the corner of the gym.

"You're starting to play unselfish basketball." He squinted from player to player and grunted, Coach's version of a compliment. "I think you're ready for something new. Something that requires real teamwork."

He explained the Eddie/Manning High-Lob-to-the-Low-Post play, the one I'd thought up. He drew out *Xs* and *Os* on the blackboard. Then we ran through the play for real.

Eddie dribbled around the perimeter. Drew all the defenders away from the basket. And you could see on his face he wanted to take the shot himself. Wanted to slice through the defense, one on five, and take the ball to the hoop.

But he controlled himself.

Manning faked to the outside. Bragger set a pick. Manning slipped in behind the defenders, ready to take the pass. The first couple of times he posted up right under the basket and just camped there. And Coach whistled him for staying in the lane too long. I pretty much expected that.

Didn't take Manning long to catch on, though. Eddie made his moves. Dribbled. Faked left. Faked right. Really looked like he was trying to find an opening through the defense. The other offensive players stayed with him. Looked like they were trying to get open. Trying to help Eddie out. Manning ran to the outside, too.

Meanwhile, Bragger set the pick, and Manning slid down to the low post. Eddie lobbed the ball. Manning caught it. Stepped into the paint. And laid it up. Two points.

A classic backdoor play. Executed perfectly.

The guys high-fived each other.

Eddie caught Coach's eye. "Excellent play, Coach."

"Yes, it is." Coach nodded. "And you can thank your captain for it. He came up with it."

Coach jogged out onto the court to set up the play again, and as he ran past, he reached out and ruffled my hair.

Twenty-four

Coach ruffled my hair. With his actual hand.

It must be a sign, I decided. A good sign. A sign that I—and the whole team—might actually come through this thing in one relatively undamaged piece.

Either that, or a sign I should quit before I made the damage permanent.

But I couldn't quit. We were too close. Too close to maybe beating Whipple. Too close to maybe having a winning season. Too close to meeting Brett McGrew.

Brett McGrew. My father. My actual father. I never thought it would happen, but here we were: *this close* to meeting my father.

And also, as Eddie pointed out Monday at lunch, way too close to playing Whipple in our skivvies.

He crunched his crackers into his chili. "We all thought Coach would come to his senses. But how long's it going to take? We don't have a lot of time here."

"Yeah," said Manning. "The Whipple game's next week."

"And we're ready for it." Eddie shoveled up a spoonful of chili and cracker crumbles. "We can take Whipple."

"Easy," said Russell.

Eddie nodded and swallowed his chili. "But we got to be wearing clothes."

"I'm not worried," said Duncan. "Kirby's got it all figured out."

I looked at him.

Duncan shrugged. "I've seen you watching Coach. And writing in your notebook. I know you're working on something."

Eddie looked from me to Duncan, then back again. "So," he said. "Whatcha got?"

"Well—"

I pulled a pencil and my notebook from my backpack. Opened the notebook and set it in the middle of the table so the team could see the two columns.

"Duncan's right," I said. "I've been watching Coach. The evidence is pretty skimpy. I don't really have enough data to support either theory. But if I had to guess, I'd go with *Coach Is Psyching Us Out.*"

Bragger nodded. "That side's winning, four to three."

"Right. Plus it just seems to make more sense. See how the first column is just a jumble of things?" I thumped my pencil against the first column. "Coach watches us carefully, he gives the technology time to kick in, he thinks the uniforms are paying off sooner than he expected. That doesn't add up to much." I moved my pencil to the second column. "But over here, you can kind of see a pattern emerging. A pattern molded around a science project. Coach studies us, gives his science experiment time to kick in, says he's created a monster, like a mad scientist or something."

The guys studied the notebook page, heads nodding. Maybe they believed me. Maybe they just wanted to believe me.

"Plus, as Duncan pointed out, Coach isn't stupid." I pointed to item number four in the second column.

I stopped. Frowned. No, Coach *wasn't* stupid. I'd forgotten one very important piece of evidence. I grabbed up the notebook and, in the second column, scribbled:

> 5. The Eddie/Manning backdoor play. If Coach really believed in Stealth technology, he wouldn't be coming up with new plays. He'd just rely on the uniforms to win the game.

I slapped the notebook back down in the middle of the table. The guys read the last piece of evidence.

"So we're his science experiment." Eddie shrugged. "I can live with that. All we have to do is wait him out."

"Easy," said Russell.

Twenty-five

It was our last practice before the Whipple game, and Coach really got into it. Literally. We were running the Eddie/Manning backdoor play, and Coach put himself into the drill. Defending Manning.

He set his clipboard on one of the bleacher seats, dropped his whistle on top, and planted himself in front of Manning, knees bent, head up, arms out. Same defensive stance he'd been drilling into our heads all season.

"If you can get around me," he growled at Manning, "you can get around anybody Whipple throws at you."

But, of course, Manning couldn't. Not at first, anyway. Even after Bragger set the pick, he couldn't shake Coach long enough to get any kind of position. He couldn't get open for the pass. Couldn't get Coach out of his face.

But we ran through the play a couple dozen times, and Manning started to put a little more space between him and his defender. Finally, the last time we ran the play, Manning lost Coach long enough to post up. Eddie lobbed the pass. Manning caught it. Coach charged into the paint to defend, but Manning laid it in. Right over Coach's head.

Manning stood there, stunned.

Coach slapped him on the back. "Nice job, Reece." He turned to the rest of the team. "Good work today. Get a good night's sleep. Tomorrow's the big day."

We filed into the locker room. Everybody, including Coach, showered and went home. I cleaned up after them, showered and changed, and snapped off the lights. I clicked the locker room door shut behind me, hiked my backpack onto my shoulder, and set off, my footsteps echoing across the dark gym.

A single knife of light beamed through a crack in the papered-over windows and sliced across a flat object lying on the bottom bench of the bleachers. Coach's clipboard. With his whistle lying on top.

"Oh, man." My whisper boomed through the empty gym.

I glanced around. What was I going to do? This was Coach's clipboard. His private clipboard. The sacred place where he kept everything important to the team. Plays. Rosters. Lineups. Scouting reports. And who knew what else. All strictly for his eyes only. He'd tie my arms in a knot if he knew I'd even touched it.

But I sure couldn't leave it lying there, unguarded, for just anybody to find.

I grabbed his whistle, then carefully picked up the clipboard, grasping the very top of the metal clip by two fingers. As I set off across the gym, a thin sheet of yellow paper slipped loose and fluttered to the floor.

Great.

I picked up the sheet. Started to clip it back onto the board, under the other papers, where it had been before. And stopped. The single knife of light landed on two words at the top of the sheet: STEALTH SPORTSWEAR.

Stealth Sportswear? I slapped the yellow paper to my chest and glanced around to make sure I really was alone. To make sure nobody else could see what I'd just seen. The gym was still empty.

I sank down onto the bleachers, dropped my backpack beside me, and peeled the paper from my chest. Held it to the light. It was a receipt. A carbon copy of a receipt for— I swallowed—twelve sets of basketball uniforms, red for away games, white for home. And one warm-up suit, adult size extra-large.

I stared at the receipt. He'd done it. He'd actually done it. It didn't matter how much evidence I'd collected to prove Coach didn't believe in Stealth technology. To prove he was using sports psychology on us. Was messing with our minds. It didn't matter that column #2 made more sense than column #1. Coach had bought invisible uniforms.

No, not invisible. Nonexistent. Coach had bought thirteen boxes of air.

And spent a lot of money on it. I looked closer. At the total circled at the bottom of the receipt. At the words PAID IN FULL stamped in red. Man. It must've been his entire basketball budget for the whole year. And he'd blown it on . . . nothing.

The receipt quivered in my hand. It was a flimsy sheet of paper, practically see-through. Didn't add up to more than a sliver of an ounce. But it was heavy enough to sink our whole basketball program. I closed my eyes. Wait till

Mrs. Zimmer found out. It was bad enough we were running around the gym naked. Wait till she found out how much all that nakedness had cost.

Well, there wasn't much I could do about it now. I slid the receipt under the other papers and made sure it was clipped tight, then carried everything back into the locker room. Coach's office was locked, of course, so I hung the clipboard and the whistle on the nail outside his door. With any luck, he'd think the janitor had left them there.

I heaved my backpack onto my shoulder and trudged from the locker room, through the empty gym, and out into the frigid November night. I pulled my coat up around my ears, leaned into the wind, and set off for home, the notebook filled with worthless evidence banging against my back.

Twenty-six

"**K**irb. Hey." Bragger jabbed me with the corner of his lunch card. "What's wrong with you?"

I looked back at him. "Well, for one thing, my shoulder's gone numb where you keep poking me."

"Besides that."

I rolled my eyes. "For the twenty-third time, nothing." I turned back to face the front of the lunch line.

"Nothing. Right. Let's recap." Bragger scootched out of line so that he was standing next to me. "During first period"—he held up one finger—"you stared straight into your math book the whole time and didn't wave your hand in the air once to answer a question. During second period"—he held up another finger—"it took you the whole class period to finish a one-page pronoun quiz. During third period"—another finger—"you had no idea where we were when Mr. Greunke called on you to read out loud. During fourth period"—another finger—"you blanked out so completely when Mrs. Van Meter asked you to demonstrate the proper way to light a Bunsen burner, that she made you sit down and had to ask Duncan—*Duncan*—to show us." He wagged his four fingers in my face. "That's not like you, Kirby."

I shrugged. "It's game day." I inched forward in line. "I'm just, you know, nervous."

136

"About?"

"About the game, Bragger. What else?"

Bragger narrowed his eyes. Studied me for a moment. "Yeah," he said. "What else?"

The rest of the team was already sitting around The Hulk when Bragger and I got there.

Eddie looked up. "Nickel." He swallowed a bite of sloppy joe. "Just the guy I was waiting for. You find more evidence?"

"Evidence?" I swallowed. My tray clattered against the table. "What kind of evidence?"

Eddie looked at me. Let out a big breath. "What kind do you think? Evidence that we're Coach's big science project. Evidence that really clinches it. Like, did he pull you aside after practice yesterday and say, 'Nickel, guess what? Those invisible uniforms? I was just kidding.' Anything like that?"

"Um." I sank into my chair. "Not exactly."

"Cause here's the thing, man." Eddie slugged back a gulp of milk, straight from the carton. He wiped the milk mustache off with the back of his hand. "We're out of time."

"Yeah," said Russell.

"Yeah," said Manning.

"Yeah." The word echoed around the table.

I glanced at my teammates. At eleven guys I'd convinced to follow me onto the basketball court wearing nothing but their underwear. Eleven guys who now wanted me, their team captain, to reassure them that their days of playing skivvy ball were over.

137

I took a deep breath. Stared down at my sloppy joe for inspiration. It just sat there waiting to be eaten. Stupid sandwich.

"Don't worry," I finally said. "Column two is still winning." Technically, it was. Five to four. "When we get to the locker room before the game, we'll suit up in our old uniforms."

"Our old uniforms?" Duncan scrunched his face into a frown. "Did Coach—"

I held up my hand. "Don't worry about Coach. Just put on the uniforms." I glanced around the table. Swallowed. Hard. "It'll be okay," I said. "Trust me."

Trust me. Right. Because I'd taken such good care of everything so far.

I checked my watch on my way out of the lunchroom: 12:06. The game started at seven sharp. That gave me six hours and fifty-four minutes to convince Coach to let us play Whipple in our old, completely detectable-by-radar, slightly frayed-but-visible-to-the-naked-eye, polyester uniforms. Polyester wouldn't make us run faster or jump higher, but polyester did conceal our undershorts and bare chests, which, no matter what Coach thought, was all you really needed in a basketball uniform. Luckily (or unluckily, depending on how many pieces my body ended up in when this was all over), I was spending the next hour with Coach. Fifth period was P.E.

I raced to the gym and found him wheeling the ball cart out of the equipment closet. I scurried over.

"Coach. Hey. I've been thinking. About the game." I lowered my voice. The rest of the class had started to filter through to the locker room. I kept my back to them. "As team captain, I feel it's my duty to safeguard any secrets, plays, game plans, or other information vital to our team. An example would be, say, our playbook. We'd never let another team see that. Right? So I was wondering, do you think we really ought to let Whipple see our Stealth Uniforms? I mean, they're our secret weapon. Shouldn't we keep them, well, secret?"

Coach finished locking the equipment closet. Turned and gave me a long look. "I'll let you in on a little secret about secret weapons, Nickel. They don't work if you don't use them." He rolled the ball cart toward me. "Get this set up for class, okay?"

"Right." I nodded. "Okay."

Strike one.

I didn't get another opportunity to talk to him till fifth period was almost over. The class lined up to shoot free throws. Coach stood off to one side, by himself, watching and making marks in his grade book.

I sidled over. "Coach." I kept my voice low. "I was thinking."

"You do a lot of that."

"Yeah." I nodded. Swallowed. "I was thinking about this old gym. It's awful drafty in here. Sometimes it can get downright, well, cold. As team captain, I feel it's my duty to protect the team's health. I'd hate for our players to catch a chill. So what I was thinking was, maybe we should layer up."

Coach glanced at me. Raised an eyebrow. "Layer up?"

"Yeah. You know. Wear our old uniforms over our new ones so we don't get cold." And here I added what I thought was a true stroke of genius. "Which will also allow us to use our secret weapon without giving up the secret. The Stealth Uniforms will be underneath, doing their job, hidden by the old uniforms on top."

"You know, Nickel, if you're getting cold in here, I must not be working you hard enough. But I can fix that." Coach folded his arms across his chest and rocked back on his heels. "Give me twenty. No . . ." He stretched his mouth into an evil-gym-teacher smile. "Make that thirty."

Thirty. Meaning laps.

I was still running circles around the gym when the bell rang. And Coach was right. I wasn't cold.

Strike two.

I didn't see Coach again till school was out. I was headed toward the gym to look for him when I saw him come out of the teacher's lounge. I bobbed and weaved my way through the packed hallway to catch up to him.

"Coach. Hey."

He glanced around. "Nickel." He didn't break his stride. "Let me guess. You've been thinking."

"Well. Yeah. And here's the thing—"

"No." Coach held up his hand. "*Here's* the thing. I've got a basketball game to get ready for. If I fall down dead or become otherwise incapacitated, you are more than welcome to take over the team. Until that time, keep your suggestions to yourself." We'd reached the gym, and now he stopped, one hand on the door. "You've got a basketball game to get ready for, too, Nickel. So quit worrying about what you're going to wear and start thinking about how you're going to play. I'm counting on you to give me your best game tonight. Got that?"

I swallowed. "Got it."

"Good." He pushed through the door and disappeared into the gym.

Strike three. Batter out.

Twenty-seven

I checked my watch: 5:47. I leaned over and checked the alarm clock by my bed: 5:47. The date and time on my computer screen: 5:47. I let out a big breath. One hour and thirteen minutes till tip-off. Thirteen minutes till the team was supposed to suit up. Thirteen minutes till life as I knew it exploded in my face.

And I admit it: I wanted to run away. Every cell in my body was screaming, "Run, Kirby, run!" I wasn't sure where I'd go. Or how I'd get there. A twenty-inch mountain bike takes you only so far in the dead of November.

Then I thought about the attic. I could live up there for years without anybody knowing. It was warm, with lots of blankets and clothes and the mattress from my old baby bed. I could tiptoe downstairs every night after Grandma fell asleep (and I'd know when she was asleep—her snores rattle the rafters) and snag enough food to keep me going for the next day. I'd have to rig up something in case I had to go to the bathroom during the day, but that wouldn't be hard. A coffee can with a lid would do the trick. I could take my Game Boy and a supply of books with me to keep from getting bored. Maybe I could even wire an Internet connection and sneak my computer up there. I could hole up in the attic, nice and cozy, without anybody wanting to hurt me, till it was time to go off to college. Just me and the giant prairie dog.

"Ready, Kirby?" Grandma appeared in my bedroom doorway, her red-and-white Stuckey booster jacket zipped to her chin. Her bleacher cushion was tucked under one arm, her big black purse slung over the other. She jangled her car keys. "We don't want to be late."

Yeah. That would be a tragedy.

The gym was a lot busier than the last time I'd seen it. Trumpet blasts drowned out clarinet squeaks as the pep band warmed up in the bleachers. The seventh-grade cheerleaders, practicing their cheers, bounced and rustled pompoms. Mr. Greunke, our social studies teacher and official scorekeeper, bustled around under the bright gym lights, directing students who were setting up the scorer's table and running cords to the sound equipment. The air was dense with noise and expectation.

Grandma immediately planted herself in the front row of the bleachers, directly behind the Stuckey bench, her usual spot during any Stuckey basketball game. Because, as she said, you never knew when the team's coach might need a little coaching himself.

Wait till she saw what *our* coach was planning.

I shuffled across the long expanse of hardwood toward the locker room. Coach was probably already in there. In his office. Suited up in his boxers, waiting for the rest of us to do the same.

143

Which was never going to happen. The guys would never do that. They'd refuse to play in their underpants, we'd forfeit the game to Whipple, Mrs. Zimmer would cancel the basketball program, we wouldn't go to Lawrence, I wouldn't meet my father, none of us would ever be able to show our faces in this town again, and the whole team—and Coach, too, probably—would end up living in the attic with me.

And there was nothing I could do to stop it. I'd tried talking to Coach. He wouldn't even listen anymore. What else could I do? Lock him in his office? Wallop him with another basketball and hope it smacked the sense back into him?

I shook my head and pushed through the locker room door, my head hanging low.

"Nickel. Man, you should've told us."

"I can't believe you kept it secret."

"Yeah," said Bragger. "Even from me."

"I know." I was still slumped over, staring at my shoes. "It's just, I couldn't. I mean . . ."

I took a deep breath. Finally looked up.

And about fell right out the door backward.

Eddie, Duncan, and Bragger had beaten me to the locker room. Eddie and Bragger were flexing and strutting in front of their lockers. Duncan was still sitting on the bench, struggling to pull his head through his jersey.

And all of them wore shiny new uniforms. White, shot through with a big red lightning bolt that started on one shoulder and zigzagged across their shirts and down their shorts to the opposite knee. The word STUCKEY stretched across the front in blocky black letters.

I blinked. "Where did those come from?"

Eddie looked at me. "Our lockers, man. Where else?"

"So you just"—I swallowed—"saw them? Suddenly?"

"Well, yeah." Duncan's head finally popped through his jersey. "And look." He turned around so I could read the back. Six letters—WEBBER—arched over a big black number thirteen. "We got our names on the back."

Manning and Russell banged in the door behind me. About knocked me over.

The rest of the team filed in behind them. And stopped short.

"Whoa," said Manning.

A grin spread across Russell's face. "Cool."

"Look in your locker," said Duncan. "There's two of them hanging there."

"White for home. Red for away." Coach's voice boomed off the concrete.

We looked up.

Coach strode from his office. Wearing a red-and-white lightning-streaked warm-up suit. Adult size extra-large.

He planted himself in the middle of the locker room. "You're looking at your new uniforms, gentlemen. Better than what you've been playing in, huh?" He raised his eyebrows. "You didn't believe in those Stealth Uniforms, did you?"

145

We looked at each other.

"Oh. No."

"No way."

We shook our heads.

Coach nodded. "Good. 'Cause those things never existed. You knew that, right?"

"Right."

"Oh, yeah."

"We knew that."

We looked at each other. Nodded.

"Funny thing about those Stealth Uniforms, though." Coach crossed his arms over his chest. Narrowed his eyes. "They worked."

We shot sideways looks at each other.

"They did exactly what I promised they'd do. Made you run faster. Jump higher. Play harder. They even pulled you together as a team. You didn't have a choice. Your coach was making you play ball in your underpanties. You *had* to stick together. Not bad for a box of air. And one more thing about those nonexistent uniforms. I told you that only true winners, only those who have what it takes to control the technology, can use them." Coach pooched out his lips. "And I was right. You boys proved it. Every single one of you is a winner. Every single one of you showed me you've got what it takes."

He nodded. Gazed from player to player.

"Now suit up," he said. "Let's show this town what we're made of."

Twenty-eight

Oh, we showed them what we were made of, all right.

We bounded into the gym in our snazzy new uniforms. And got hit by a freight train of noise. Pep band. Pep club. Cheerleaders. Spectators packed into the bleachers— Whipple, a wall of green T-shirts and ball caps, on one end; Stuckey, in red, crammed elbow to elbow at the other. Mrs. Zimmer, straight and tall, sat in the front row, a few seats down from Grandma.

The Stuckey fans whistled and cheered as we trotted over to our side of the court to start stretching and warming up. Whipple fans blew armpit farts. I wasn't surprised. You learn to expect that kind of thing from Whipple.

I sprawled on the floor to stretch my calf muscles. And tried to look cool and casual. On the outside, anyway.

The other guys weren't doing much better. Oh, sure, Bragger and Eddie did a good job of faking it. They smirked and swaggered and acted like they'd never missed a shot in their lives. And sneaked panicked, sideways glances at Mrs. Zimmer when they thought nobody was looking. And didn't sneak any glances at all at the seventh-grade cheerleaders in their flippy skirts, which was a dead giveaway, especially where Eddie was concerned.

Russell practiced his game face. He scowled at the

Whipple players warming up at the other end of the court and let out mini–Coach growls from time to time. And wiped the palms of his hands on his shorts, leaving nervous streaks of sweat across the shiny new polyester.

Duncan didn't even attempt a game face. He sidled up next to me as I sat hunched over on the floor, stretching my hamstrings.

"Kirby?" His voice was weak and wavery. His face, freakishly pale under normal circumstances, had taken on a gray tinge. "I think I'm going to throw up."

"I know." I switched legs so I could stretch the other hamstring. "Me, too. Keep telling yourself it's just pregame jitters. That's what I'm doing."

We finished stretching and warming up. Coach gathered us beside the row of scuffed metal folding chairs that was our bench.

He consulted his clipboard. "Starting lineup: Reece, Poggemeyer, Barnes, Webber, and Nickel."

"Nickel?" I stared at him. "You mean Wiles. Russell Wiles."

Coach looked at me. "When I mean Wiles, I *say* Wiles. When I say Nickel, I mean you. You're in."

"But I'm—I'm—"

"You're the most consistent player on this team."

Oh, boy. That lightning bolt across his warm-up suit must've sucked all the juice from his brain.

"This is a joke, right?" I inched over next to him. Kept my voice low. "I know you're kidding, because, as I'm sure

148

you've noticed, I'm not exactly starting lineup material. I have no discernible athletic skill. I've got to be the least-talented person to ever set foot in this gym."

"Yep." Coach nodded. "You probably are. But you've done more with less natural ability than anybody I've seen since, well, since me."

He narrowed his eyes. Studied me. "I'll let you in on a little secret, Nickel," he said finally. He turned his back so the other guys couldn't hear. "I wasn't a born athlete, any more than you are. But I wanted it more than anybody. I turned myself into a basketball player through sheer bullheadedness. And I see that same bullheadedness in you. The way you dive for every rebound. Drive to the hoop when you get the ball. Push yourself relentlessly every minute of every practice."

Yeah. Push myself to dislocate a limb.

"You've worked harder than anybody on the team," he said. "Developed skills you weren't meant to have. I never thought I'd say this, Nickel, but you're a solid player. And you're starting, so get your fanny over there." He turned to Russell. "Sit here next to me on the bench, Wiles. You're my sixth man. I'm counting on you to give us valuable minutes."

Russell nodded and scooted onto the metal folding chair next to Coach.

The buzzer honked.

I stumbled onto the floor. As a starter. My worst nightmare.

And, at the same time, my secret dream come true. I'd never said this out loud. Not to Grandma. Not to Bragger. Not even to myself. But deep down inside, so deep I hardly let myself think about it, I had dreamed of this moment. Of being good enough to nail a starting spot. Even during those weeks when I was doing everything I knew to sprain a vital body part so I wouldn't have to play, even then, in the darkest corner of my heart, I was wondering what it would be like to trot onto the floor as a starter. I was Brett McGrew's son, after all. Wouldn't it be cool if I could actually play?

The buzzer honked again. Game time.

The crowd noise quieted to a dull rumble. Mr. Greunke announced the starting lineups and we took our positions around the circle. Manning faced off against the Whipple center.

Manning had at least two inches on the Whipple guy. And his arms looked longer. Manning was built like a gorilla—big, bony knuckles dangling from long, lanky arms. Plus he'd been working on his jump. In practice he'd been vaulting a good two feet off the floor, which, for Manning, was like leaping a tall building in a single bound.

So tip-off looked good. Looked like a part of the game where we could hold our own.

Until, of course, the ref actually tossed the ball into the air, and Manning just hunkered there in his ready position. Didn't jump. Didn't try to hit the ball. Just crouched there like a paralyzed seventh-grade gorilla.

Meanwhile, the Whipple center batted the ball to the Whipple two guard, who pushed it up court and—*tha-bump*—sank an easy layup. Before any of our players had even made it down the court.

"Shake it off, guys," Coach hollered as Bragger inbounded the ball to Eddie. "We'll get that basket back. Manning, be ready. This is your play."

Well, it would've been his play. Except that Eddie couldn't get the ball across the midcourt line before his ten seconds were up. The ref blew his whistle. And Whipple had the ball.

Again.

The game skidded downhill from there.

We couldn't get it together on defense. Manning lost his man immediately. Duncan basically knew where his man was, but, being Duncan, that didn't mean he could keep up with him. Eddie dogged his man. Just dogged him. Hands in his face. Hips blocking him out. Feet sliding. Dogged him like, well, like a dog. Until Whipple set a screen and Eddie got turned around and ended up dogging Bragger.

We couldn't get it together on offense, either. Whipple pulled off four steals when Duncan, in a panic, started passing to the first open man he saw. Sadly, the open man was usually wearing a green jersey. And every time we set up the Manning play, we might as well have handed the ball over to Whipple. Manning got under the basket, all right. He got under the basket and stayed.

And stayed.

And stayed.

Could have pitched a tent and set out a lawn chair, that's how long he stayed.

He racked up eight three-second violations in eight minutes. Coach tried to get our heads into the game. He called time-outs. He mapped out plays. He gave pep talks. He set goals: "For the next three minutes, let's concentrate on cutting their lead in half." He substituted Wiles for Reece and Reece for Poggemeyer and Poggemeyer for Wiles.

But we still played in a fog. One step behind Whipple on every possession.

The buzzer sounded. Halftime. Finally. I'd been trying not to look at the scoreboard while we were playing, but there was no avoiding it now. I glanced up. Whipple 34, Stuckey 8.

The wave of green T-shirts cheered the Whipple players and armpit farted the Stuckey players. The Stuckey fans shook their heads and made their way toward the concession stand. Mrs. Zimmer marched behind them, her nostrils flared, probably to let off the steam that was no doubt boiling her brain.

Our guys trudged toward the locker room.

Twenty-nine

Coach tossed his clipboard. It skidded across the bench and clattered to the floor. He ran both hands through his buzz cut. Paced toward his office and back.

Finally, he looked at us. Looked from player to player. Looked hard.

"Who *are* you people?" He choked out a growl. "You're not the players I coached in practice. You're not the players who sweated their buns off every day, behind locked doors and taped-over windows. You're not the players who went from ball hogging and lazy defense to actually working as a team."

He strode to the chalkboard. Grabbed a piece of chalk and started drawing out *X*s and *O*s. He stopped. Shook his head. And threw the chalk back down.

"No. You know what? I'm not going to do this. I could stand here all day drawing out plays. Showing you where you should have been and what you should've been doing. But you know all of it already. It's what you've been doing in practice every single day. That's the frustrating part. The players I know, the players I've seen in practice, could beat this Whipple team. Because Whipple's not that good. They made their share of mistakes. One of their forwards got into foul trouble early because of stupid reach-ins and had to sit most of the half on the bench. Their shooting guard isn't much of a shooter. He thinks he is. He takes a lot of shots. Hardly any go in. If we'd been rebounding at all, we could've put up a whole lot more shots of our own. But you know what? That shooting guard isn't afraid to try. He's not like you." He swept his arm toward the team. "You all are just plain scared. And I can't draw out a single play that can fix it. That's something you're going to have to fix yourselves."

He snatched his clipboard from the floor, stalked into his office, and slammed the door.

We slumped on the bench in silence, watching Coach's miniblinds rattle against the glass.

I glanced at the players. Coach was right. We were playing scared. The whole team was playing like I'd always played. Not scared of striking out or getting tackled or missing a shot, exactly. Scared of what people would think of me when I *did* strike out or get tackled or miss a shot. Scared people would think I was stupid. Scared spitless of looking stupid.

"Well, we sure look stupid out there tonight."

I didn't know I'd even spoken out loud till Eddie said, "No kidding. We didn't look *that* stupid when we were playing naked."

I nodded.

Then stared at him.

"You're right," I said. "You're totally right."

Eddie looked at me. Suspiciously. "Yeah. So?"

"So." I turned to Duncan. "The first time we walked into the gym in our underwear, how did you feel?"

154

Duncan swallowed. Glanced nervously at the guys. "Naked. Embarrassed." He shrugged. "Cold."

"And scared?"

"Scared out of my pants. Except I wasn't wearing any."

"We were all scared." I looked at the other guys, who nodded. "But we did it anyway. And then we started playing basketball. Better than we ever had before. How come?"

Eddie shrugged. "Nothing left to lose."

"Right." I stood up. "We were as embarrassed as we were ever going to get. We didn't care if we looked stupid, because guess what?" I untucked my lightning-bolt jersey. "We already looked stupid. Our uniforms took care of that. All that was left was basketball. So we played."

I pulled my jersey over my head and tossed it into my locker. I peeled off my snazzy new lightning-bolt shorts, tossed them in, too, and stood there, in the middle of the locker room, in nothing but my gym shoes and underwear.

"Uh, Kirby? Kirb?" Bragger glanced at the other guys out of the corners of his eyes. "What are you doing?"

I shrugged. "You've heard of players being superstitious? Players who, if they're not playing well, change their shoes at halftime? Coaches who change their tie? Well, I'm beyond superstitious. I'm changing my whole uniform. In the second half, I'm going Stealth."

The guys stared at me. Mouths open, nothing coming out. Paralyzed by shock, I imagine.

Duncan, surprisingly, recovered first.

He stood up on wobbly legs. "I want to play better in the second half, too." He wriggled out of his jersey, then

155

his shorts. He came over and stood beside me. "I'm going Stealth."

Eddie shook his head. "Man. You two are dorky enough as it is. You don't need to help it along."

"Hey!" Duncan took a step toward him, fists clenched. "We're not dorky."

"Yes, we are, Duncan. We're the two biggest dorks on the team. And guess what?" I pinned Eddie with a steady gaze. "The dorks aren't afraid to walk out into that gym in their underwear."

Duncan looked at me. Swallowed. "Well, this dork kind of is."

"I know. Me, too." I gave Duncan an encouraging punch in the arm. "But the point is, we're doing it anyway." I turned to the other guys. "We dorks may be scared, but we're walking out that door, we're taking our places on the court, and we're playing better basketball in the second half than anybody on either team. In our underwear."

"Hey." Bragger stood up. "Don't leave me out." He tugged his jersey over his head. "I'm a dork, too. And if I can take it—"

"Oh, man." Russell shook his head. "If you can take it, I can take it." He slid his shirt over his head.

"I can, too," said Manning.

One by one, the guys pulled off their uniforms. One by one, they came over to stand in the Stealth huddle.

Eddie looked at us. Rolled his eyes to the ceiling. "God. We're all dorks," he said. And he peeled off his jersey.

Thirty

"What is going on here?"

Coach's voice ricocheted off the lockers.

About knocked us flat. We froze. We'd kind of forgotten about him.

He strode across the cement. "What are you doing? We have to be out on the court in two minutes. And you're changing clothes?" He stopped. "Don't tell me. You're not just giving up. Changing into your street clothes and going home." He whirled on me. "Nickel?"

"Uh, no, sir. We're not giving up. We're, well, we're ready for the second half."

Coach scrunched his face into a frown. Raised an eyebrow. Looked at me like my brain had just turned to slush and leaked out my ear.

I took a deep breath. "You said it yourself, Coach. Stealth Uniforms made us run faster, jump higher, play longer. They turned us into a team."

Duncan's voice squeaked. "And you also said you couldn't fix our scaredness. We had to fix it ourselves."

Coach narrowed his eyes. Ran a hand across his forehead. "And this is what you came up with?"

We swallowed. Nodded.

"And you were just going to waltz out there and make me look stupid?"

Oh, man. We hadn't even thought about that. About how our nakedness would embarrass Coach.

"Because I *would* look stupid, believe me, if I was the only one on the bench fully dressed."

He shook his head and unzipped his warm-up jacket. He wriggled out of it. He tossed his pants on the bench. He tucked his clipboard under his hairy arm-pit, squared his bare shoulders, and marched toward the door.

We followed Coach out of the locker room and across the court, our goose bumps gleaming under the buzzing gym lights.

Nobody noticed us at first. Folks were still wandering back from the concession stand, finding their seats. Their voices rumbled through the big, hollow gym.

But then one fan, and another, and another, glanced down. Pointed us out to their neighbors. Everybody stared at us, stared at our underwear, stared at each other. The gym went silent.

Then folks started giggling. One by one. It started on the Whipple end, of course. Whipple fans have always been bad sports. But it didn't take long to spread, and pretty soon even the Stuckey fans were laughing. First a snicker, then a chuckle, then a couple of guffaws, till the whole gym erupted in howls.

And we just stood there and took it.

The officials and the Whipple coach came racing over, of course. Swarmed Coach. Wanted to know what we were up to. What kind of mind game we were playing. Paged through the league regulations, trying to figure out

158

how many rules we were breaking.

Now, Coach was a lot of things, but nobody could ever call him chicken. He stood right up to those referees and that coach, as cool and confident as if he'd been wearing a bulletproof Superman suit.

"We're not up to a thing," he said. "And we're not breaking any rules. I've checked. Surely you've seen a game of shirts and skins. It's a basketball tradition. We're just taking it to another level. Now if you gentlemen will excuse me, I have a game to coach."

He turned on his heel and strode back to the bench, whipped out his clipboard, just like he always did at practice, just like he would have if he'd been wearing clothes, and gathered the team for a second-half huddle.

After what seemed like a day and a half, the crowd finally settled into their seats. They stopped laughing, for the most part, but they were still talking, and not about Lloyd Metcalf's fancy new combine, either. I sneaked a glance at the bleachers. There sat Mrs. Zimmer, straight and tall, her face purple with rage, her body paralyzed with humiliation.

The buzzer honked. I tugged the legs of my boxer briefs to make sure they were covering up everything they were supposed to cover and joined my teammates at center court.

"Well," I said, "we look as stupid as we're ever going to look. No matter what we do from this point on, we can't be any more humiliated than we are right now."

"All that's left," said Bragger, "is basketball."

Eddie nodded. "Let's play!"

Thirty-one

So we played.

Manning inbounded to Eddie to start the half. Then, while Eddie dribbled around the perimeter, drawing defenders, Manning faked to the outside, then drifted toward the basket and set up in the low post, just like we'd practiced. And, just like in practice, Eddie faked right, reversed left, and executed a smooth pass over the defense. Manning caught the pass, pivoted into the paint, and put the ball through the hoop. Two points. Four seconds into the first half, and Stuckey was on the board.

And even though we were playing in our underwear, even though we were the biggest embarrassment the town had ever endured, Stuckey fans cheered. They couldn't help themselves. This was the Basketball Capital of Kansas, after all, and the citizens had to root for their team. Even Mrs. Zimmer. Her face was still purple with rage. But she clapped.

Whipple inbounded. Their point guard dribbled downcourt, Eddie in his face the whole way. The guard broke left. Ran into Eddie. Swung right. Eddie was there. Stopped and brought the ball overhead for a pass. Eddie flicked it away, recovered it in one bounce, and charged up the court for an easy layup. Two points.

Eddie pumped his fist.

Coach swung his clipboard in the air. "Nice move, Poggemeyer!"

Stuckey fans leaped to their feet, cheering.

And we kept on playing.

Manning was a maniac in the post. After Whipple caught on and began guarding him, the Maniac just started going over the defender's head for the basket, the way he'd gone over Coach's in practice.

For Duncan, the free-throw line truly was a charity stripe. Whipple had figured out that Big D wasn't the quickest player on the team. That he was vulnerable. So they double-teamed him every time he got the ball, trying to force a turnover. But Duncan was patient. He'd wait till they were all over him, hands in his face. Then he'd lob the ball in the general direction of the basket. And draw a foul. And then sink the free throws. He went ten for ten from the foul line.

Every player in a Stealth Uniform was playing great basketball.

Every player except me. I couldn't get open. Couldn't get a rebound. Couldn't get a look at the basket.

"What's wrong with you, Nickel?" Coach yelled. "If this were practice, you'd be crashing the boards, diving for loose balls."

Yeah, I wanted to yell back, because if this were practice, I'd be trying to break my neck so I wouldn't have to play.

And that's when it hit me. Coach said I was the most consistent player on the team. But I didn't get that way trying to play basketball. I'd gotten that way trying to *avoid* playing basketball.

So I just quit. Quit trying to play. Instead, I poured all my effort, once again, into spraining my ankle. My amazing, indestructible ankle. And within five minutes, I'd pulled down four rebounds, blocked three shots, and stolen the ball twice. I even put up three shots. Two of them actually dropped in.

By the end of the third quarter, we'd cut Whipple's lead in half: Whipple 46, Stuckey 33. Stuckey fans seemed to have forgotten we were playing in our undies. And we did, too. Well, almost. But the fans cheered, and we played.

And kept on playing. With one minute left in the game, we'd sliced Whipple's lead to two. Just two points. One basket. And sixty seconds left to play.

We traded the next two buckets. Bragger made a sweet little finger roll under the basket to tie. Whipple made a layup to go ahead again. The fans—both Stuckey and Whipple—were on their feet, screaming.

The clock ticked down. Sixteen seconds. And we had the ball. We had to make at least one basket. Two points. And then we'd be tied. We'd be in overtime. We'd have another shot at beating them.

Our best strategy was to get Duncan to the free-throw line, get the ball into Duncan's hands immediately, and try to get him fouled. So Eddie inbounded, and Duncan took it up the court, a risky move because Duncan had only ten seconds to get it over the line, and he wasn't what you'd call quick. He was also facing full-court pressure from two big Whipple guys who were determined not to lose this game in the final seconds.

But Big D took a deep breath, jutted his jaw, and kept dribbling. Slow and steady. Those Whipple guys were all over him, but he didn't cave. Didn't do anything crazy. Just kept moving up court.

Whipple wasn't taking any chances, either. They had their hands up, their bodies in Duncan's way, but they were being careful. They didn't want to put Duncan on the free-throw line.

Still, they were looking for their chance. And when Duncan wiped the sweat from his eyes with his free hand, they took it. The Whipple point guard swiped at the ball. Didn't touch Duncan. Didn't even come close. Just knocked the ball back.

Square into Duncan's bare, lathered-up belly. Square onto his belly button, where the suction was the greatest. Where, for a split second, the ball stayed stuck.

And I have to give Duncan credit. He didn't panic. Didn't move his feet. Didn't travel, like he did that time in practice. He couldn't dribble anymore, so he just stopped. Kept his pivot foot firmly planted. And if those two Whipple players would've just left him alone, he probably would've been called for not getting the ball over the line in time. But when Big D wrapped his arms around the ball and pivoted, trying to yank it loose, it caught the Whipple point guard off balance, and he walloped Duncan in the side with his elbow. The ball tore loose with a big *slurp* and bounced out of bounds.

The ref whistled the Whipple guard for a foul.

And Duncan was at the free-throw line with seven seconds left. Two shots. One point apiece. If he made them both, we'd be tied.

We lined up on either side of the paint. The ref threw Duncan the basketball. Duncan squared his feet. Bounced the ball. Bounced again. Lined his hands up on the stripes, eyed the basket, and—

—*whoosh.*

Nothing but net.

Stuckey fans cheered. The green wall went silent.

We all high-fived Big D, then lined up again. Whipple's lead was down to one.

The ref tossed Duncan the ball. Duncan squared. Bounced. Bounced again. Lined up his hands. Eyed the basket. Shot.

The ball soared over the paint in a perfect arc. Perfect . . . perfect . . . perfect . . .

. . . until it thudded against the bracket, spun around the rim, and bounced out.

We weren't ready for that. Weren't ready for Duncan to miss his first free throw of the half. We moved a split second too late.

The Whipple center rebounded and passed to the

Whipple point guard, who dribbled down court.

"*No-o-o-o-o!*"

I charged after him, after the ball. They weren't going to play keep-away, let the clock run out, rip this game from our grasp by one measly point. Not while there was time left. Not if I had anything to say about it.

Eddie was already in the guard's face, hands up, body pressing in, and now I was all over him, too. The guard stopped. Pivoted. Held the ball over his head to pass. Eddie leaped and tipped it loose.

Tipped it over the guard's head. Tipped it into my chest. I slapped my hands over it. I had it. I had the ball.

"Shoot, Kirby, *shoot!*" Bragger's voice echoed through the rafters.

I turned and dribbled. Dribbled and dribbled and dribbled, for miles it seemed, until I couldn't feel my arm, couldn't feel my hand pumping up and down, couldn't feel the nubby roughness of the ball. Somewhere in the outer reaches of my mind I heard the ball bouncing, heard my Jammers pounding over the wood—*thonk, thwap, thonk, thwap*—as the crowd roared. But my brain, my body, my whole self zeroed in on one thing: the basket. Put the ball in the basket.

I was almost there when I caught a flash of green out of the corner of my eye. The Whipple guard charged past and positioned himself in front of me. Positioned himself to block the shot. I glanced over. Looked for a Stuckey player, Eddie or Bragger, even Duncan, anybody in a Stealth

165

Uniform to pass to. But I was by myself. Just me and the Whipple guard. And one of us had to win.

The Whipple guard was set. If I went in for the layup, I'd plow right into him. I'd get called for a charging foul. I took my last step toward him and pulled the ball up. But instead of going straight in, I pushed off and spun away, my back to the basket. Kept spinning, lifting the ball, till I faced the basket on the other side. And laid it in.

Th-bumpf.

The ball banked off the backboard and fell through the hoop.

The buzzer honked.

The crowd exploded.

The ref threw his arm in the air. The shot was good.

Thirty-two

The Stuckey seventh-grade Prairie Dogs led off the ten o'clock Live-Action News on Channel 7 that night. We were the very first story, beating out a tax increase, a slump in wheat prices, and the weather.

"Wow," said Bragger. "Underwear basketball is bigger news than we thought."

The Channel 7 sports guy interviewed Mrs. Zimmer. She sat straight and tall in her school board president's chair, and the way her nostrils twitched at the camera every time the sports guy mentioned Mike Armstrong, you could tell she was aching to fire Coach on the spot. And send his whole team to reform school. And, while she was at it, cancel seventh-grade basketball till the NBA froze over.

But she could hardly do that right there on Channel 7, with the reporter cheerfully asking her how it felt to be a leading citizen in a town that had produced not one, but two basketball wonders: Brett McGrew and the Armstrong Coaching Method.

At the words "Armstrong Coaching Method," Mrs. Zimmer's twitch snapped into a snarl. But she recovered quickly, pulling her lips into what passed as a smile, and said, as graciously as she could through gritted teeth, "Here in Stuckey, we've always known how special our basketball program is. What Coach Armstrong did tonight doesn't surprise me."

"At least she didn't cancel us," said Bragger.

"Not so far," I said.

We made the paper that weekend, and not just in Hutchinson and Great Bend, either. The Wichita paper ran a story about us, and once again we landed on the front page of the Kansas City *Star* sports section, which Cousin Mildred thoughtfully clipped out and mailed to us.

The *Star* called Coach creative and daring. It said that in stripping his players down to their jockey shorts, Coach was literally stripping the game of basketball down to its essentials. That by getting rid of outside distractions, he was allowing his players to focus on the fundamentals. By peeling away everything but their skivvies, he had fused those players into a team. Pretty much the same stuff we'd already read in the other papers. But the end of the article was something new:

> Coach Armstrong was Brett McGrew's teammate on two state champion basketball teams. He graduated the year before McGrew led Stuckey to a remarkable third straight championship. Armstrong still holds the Kansas high school record for most steals in a single season.

"Most steals?" I stared at the article, then at Bragger, who was scrunched up next to me at the kitchen table, reading over my shoulder. "It was Coach. The guy with the most steals was Coach."

"Yeah." Bragger wrinkled his forehead. "But that doesn't make any sense. I thought Coach asked *you* who had the most steals. If it was him, why would he go around asking other people about it? Wouldn't he remember his own record?"

"He remembered. He just wanted to see if anybody else did. And they didn't." I shook my head. "Wouldn't that be awful? To do something great like set a state record, and not have anybody in your own town remember?"

Bragger wrinkled his forehead again. "But see, that doesn't make sense either. People in the Basketball Capital of Kansas would remember if one of their own players set a state record. Wouldn't they?"

I considered this. "Not if that player was on the same team as Brett McGrew. Think about it. Everything was focused on McNet, right? Everybody was watching him, waiting to see what kind of amazing shot he'd put up next. Probably nobody even noticed that other guy making all those steals."

Bragger nodded. "Especially since those steals meant McNet got to put up more shots."

We'd beaten Whipple, and Mrs. Zimmer hadn't canceled our program. Yet. But we still had lots of basketball left to play—and lots of games left to win—if we wanted to go to Lawrence.

So we kept playing. In our underwear. We'd gotten semi-famous for it, so we couldn't very well stop.

Besides, underwear basketball was working for us. Our tightie whities had helped us beat Whipple, and over the next three weeks, they helped us beat Collison, Woodard, and Pierce City. I can't say we actually got comfortable waltzing into a crowded gymnasium showing that much skin. Especially during the tournament at St. Agnes Academy, over in Lovellette, where the scorekeeper, one of the refs, and the St. Agnes coach were all nuns. But we took a deep breath, closed our eyes, and marched onto the court anyway.

By the middle of December, we were 6 and 0 and were the reigning St. Agnes Academy tournament champs.

Mrs. Zimmer kept a low profile. We hadn't seen—or, more importantly, heard—much out of her since we beat Whipple. But word around the beauty shop was that she'd ordered a brand new Jayhawk bleacher cushion.

"And not just a cheapo vinyl pad, either," Duncan told us. "A real stadium seat, with a reclining back rest and hooks to slide it in place. Not the kind of thing you'd order if you were bent on canceling a basketball program."

As we racked up wins, we also racked up fame, and not just in Kansas. News stations across the country started reporting on the remarkable success of the Armstrong Coaching Method. We showed up on ESPN, on the cover of *Sports Illustrated,* and on *David Letterman* as the number one reason to buy boxers, not briefs.

USA Today reported that teams across the country were trying their luck with underwear basketball. First, a middle school in Montana, then one in Kentucky. Pretty soon, a high school popped up in Vermont. A junior college team from the Oklahoma panhandle drove up to watch us play one night, and the next thing we heard, they were playing skivvy ball, too.

Right before Christmas, *Good Morning, America* sent their weather guy to Stuckey to do his weather broadcast. The whole town, it seemed, gathered at the Double Dribble that morning.

Grandma made a cake for the occasion. Shaped like a Jayhawk. Enormous, of course. She had to bake it in sections, and each section was lopsided, so the Jayhawk came out flat and crispy in some places, bulging in others. The car ride from our house hadn't done the frosting any good, so by the time we arrived at the Double Dribble, his yellow beak had glopped down to rest on his buckled shoes.

Manning's dad brought a Basketball Capital of Kansas cap for the weather guy, compliments of Reece Feed and Grain. Mrs. Snodgrass served the whole TV crew French vanilla cappuccino. On the house. I about fell off my chair. Mrs. Snodgrass never gave away free food. Ever. I'd seen her chase down the street after arthritic old farmers who'd forgotten to leave change on the table for their coffee. But there she was, passing out free cappuccino and smiling so wide, her crayoned eyebrows about popped off her forehead.

Coach, as usual, wasn't very talkative. "Really, not much to tell," he said when the weather guy asked how he'd developed the Armstrong Coaching Method. Which was about all Coach ever said.

But the coffee drinkers were happy to weigh in.

"It was bound to happen," said Lloyd Metcalf. "This is a basketball town, and if somebody's going to put a new wrinkle in the game, why, we pretty much expect it to happen here. This is where Brett McGrew came up with his most famous move, you know. The spinning layup."

The weatherman nodded. "Yes, Brett McGrew is quite famous for that move." He smiled into the camera. "Of course, I should remind viewers that Brett McGrew wasn't the first player to spin while doing a layup."

Which pretty much amounted to treason in Stuckey. Nobody ever said Brett McGrew wasn't the first at anything. Not inside the city limits. Not if they wanted to stick around for any length of time.

But Lloyd Metcalf just chuckled. "No, sir, he wasn't. He wasn't the first, and he wasn't the last. But he sure was the best. Still is." He pushed his Allis-Chalmers cap back and scratched his head. "Now that I think on it, McNet wasn't even the first player from Stuckey to use that move." He turned to the other coffee drinkers. "What was that other kid's name, one that did the spinning layup before Brett McGrew got ahold of it? Was that the Lamprey kid?"

The other coffee drinkers furrowed their brows and leaned over their coffee cups to ponder the question.

"Now that you mention it, I do seem to remember somebody...."

"But I thought it was Bert Hager's boy."

"Or one of the Doolins."

"Nah. Weren't none of them quick enough."

But America wasn't interested in some long-ago nobody who maybe did a spinning layup one time in the middle of nowhere, so while the coffee drinkers tried to puzzle out the player's name, the weather guy drifted over to interview Mrs. Snodgrass about her autographed Brett McGrew menu.

I glanced at Coach. A long-ago somebody who'd set a state record while nobody was looking.

"Are they right?" I said. "Did somebody really do Brett McGrew's spinning layup first?"

Coach gave a one-shoulder shrug. "Spinning in the air isn't anything new."

"So who was it?" I said.

"Doesn't matter."

"Yes, it does. I imagine it matters a lot to the person who did it."

Coach snorted. "Every player who ever put on a Stuckey uniform could've done a spinning layup, Nickel. It wouldn't matter. McNet's the one who took it places." He took a sip of coffee. "Nobody else ever went anywhere."

Thirty-three

Coach, the team, and the whole town spent the winter thinking about nothing but basketball. Me, I had something else to worry about.

I'd gone through all the trophy cases and yearbooks at the middle school and high school, every back issue of the *Full Court Press* at the library downtown, and every Internet page that showed up on every search engine I'd ever heard of till I couldn't bend my mouse finger anymore. And I still hadn't found that little part of Brett McGrew that looked like me. That one piece of visual evidence that would convince Brett McGrew in an instant that he was my father.

"Don't worry about it," Bragger told me.

It was a week before the KU game, and we were in the locker room after practice. The other guys were still showering.

Bragger snapped me with his towel. "You've still got his old number 5 jersey and the medal you found in the prairie dog. That'll grab his attention. And then you can tell him who you are. It'll work out great."

"Yeah," I said. "Great."

I moped past Coach's office to the big trash can in the corner. Coach had his door open. He was hunkered over his desk, sorting through the mountain of papers stacked in his in-box. He glanced up. Saw me starting to bag up the trash.

"Nickel." He motioned his head toward the heaped-over wastebasket by his desk. "You mind taking this out? I don't think I've emptied it since school started."

I scrambled into his office, retrieved his trash can, and dumped it into the big can out in the locker room. I had to shake it a couple of times to get the crunched-up trash in the bottom to fall out, and when I did, a wad of paper tumbled to the floor. I picked it up. Started to toss it into the can with the rest of the trash. But then something caught my eye. A big number 5.

I glanced up at Coach. He was still hunkered over his desk, leafing through a sports catalog, not paying any attention to me. I turned my back to him and unwadded the paper.

It was a picture. Torn haphazardly from a newspaper. Slightly yellowed. I smoothed it out with my hand.

And stared down at Brett McGrew. At a game shot of McNet skidding across the floor on his stomach after a loose ball, his arms outstretched. The word STUCKEY and a big number 5 were stretched across the back of his jersey, and the bottoms of his shorts were hiked up so you could see an obscene amount of bare skin.

And there, on the back of his left leg, right where his thigh met his butt cheek, was a birthmark.

A big, humiliating, heart-shaped birthmark.

"Bragger." I kept my voice low and even. Motioned for him to follow me.

We strolled—casually—around the end of the lockers, where nobody could see us. I held up the picture.

Bragger looked at it. Then at me.

He smiled. "We finally found that tiny little piece of Brett McGrew that looks like you." He punched my arm. "Too bad it had to be the most embarrassing part."

After practice, we stopped by the drugstore so I could buy another roll of film.

Back home, in the safety of my bedroom, I put on the number 5 Stuckey High School basketball uniform from my mother's dresser. I had to pull the shorts up practically to my armpits and fix them with a safety pin so they wouldn't fall down around my ankles. But once Bragger finished fluffing me out and making sure I wasn't crooked, it didn't look too bad. Especially not from the back, which is what we were most concerned with.

"Got the ball?" said Bragger.

I nodded and thumped my autographed Jayhawk basketball.

"Okay, get into position."

We'd pushed my rug aside so that the bare wood floor would show, simulating a basketball court. I hiked the leg of my shorts up, stretched out on my stomach, and pretended I was reaching for the ball. Bragger kicked my feet apart so they were in the same position as Brett McGrew's in the picture.

"Perfect," he said.

"Does the birthmark show?"

"Oh, yeah. Big and heart shaped, just like McNet's."He clicked the picture.

By the time the season rolled to a close, the Stuckey Prairie Dogs were 14 and 0 and had won the league championship for the first time since Brett McGrew played seventh-grade ball. The nearly bare championship banner hanging in the middle school gym now had one more year stitched onto it: ours.

Nobody could argue with success like that, not even Mrs. Zimmer. So early one wind-whipped February morning, a Stuckey school bus pulled out of the middle-school parking lot, the seventh-grade basketball team and its coach on board, and rumbled up Highway 50 toward Lawrence.

Thirty-four

I'd heard about it all my life. I'd seen it on TV and had posters of it lining my bedroom walls. And now I was actually here. In Allen Fieldhouse, home of the Jayhawks.

The lights, the noise, the sheer size of the place made me dizzy. I stood at the edge of the court, holding my fat brown envelope carefully by the edges so I wouldn't crinkle anything inside. I gazed up at the arena. At the thousands of seats. At the enormous cube of a scoreboard poised over center court. At the banners. All those crimson and blue championship banners. We thought we'd really beefed up the Stuckey Middle School banner when we added one more year, but ours looked downright scroungy compared to the ones hanging from the ceiling of Allen Fieldhouse. Conference championships. Final Four appearances. National championships. I thought the rafters would sag from the sheer weight of them.

Bragger elbowed me. "There's Wilt."

He pointed toward the tiny windows up by the rafters, to a row of retired jerseys lining the walls behind the nosebleed seats about a mile above my head. And there it was. A big blue jersey, number 13, with CHAMBERLAIN stitched across the back.

I clutched my envelope and stood there, staring. Goose bumps ran up my arms. It was like the place was haunted. Haunted by greatness.

Eddie bumped into me. "Hey, man. Don't just stand there like a jockstrap."

"Yeah, Kirby." Russell grinned and jabbed me with his elbow. "Move out of the way."

They pushed past, along with the rest of the team. I smoothed the edges of my envelope and turned to follow. The school board had sprung for new warm-up suits, so as we snaked through the crowd and around the cheerleaders, we were easy to spot: twelve seventh-grade basketball players and their coach, all in matching red with a lightning bolt that streaked diagonally across our jacket and down our pants. We all had matching boxers on underneath, too. Silky white with little Jayhawks printed all over.

Our seats were three rows from the floor, behind the Jayhawk bench. Mrs. Zimmer and Mr. Dobbs were already sitting at the end of the row, waiting. Grandma had somehow managed to snag a seat beside them, even though she wasn't an official representative of the Stuckey school district.

The team circled the court to the wooden steps that led to our seats. I'd just started up behind Bragger when I heard a familiar grunt behind me. I turned around.

Coach was standing there, one foot poised above the first step, staring at the row of folding chairs at the edge of the court. At the Jayhawk bench, empty now, the players still in the locker room preparing for the game.

He rubbed his hand slowly across his mouth. "Always thought I'd sit there," he said, to himself, I think. "I'd wear a Jayhawk jersey, and I'd sit on that bench."

He took a deep breath and just stood there, staring at those seats, his foot hovering in midair.

"So do it," I said.

He cut his eyes toward me, surprised, I think, that anyone had heard him. "Do what?"

"Sit on the bench," I said. "Be a Jayhawk for a few minutes."

Coach narrowed his eyes. Glanced at the yellow-vested security guards milling about the floor. "I doubt security'd be real happy if I just plopped myself down on the home bench."

"So?" I shrugged. Playing basketball in boxer briefs had given me a reckless streak. "What are they going to do? Throw you out? A guest of honor? I don't think so." I motioned my head toward the bench. "Just do it."

Coach looked at me. Then at the folding chairs. A smile threatened to break out at the corners of his mouth. "You come with me."

"Me?"

"Yeah. We'll both be Jayhawks."

I glanced around. The yellow vests weren't paying any attention to us. Neither was Mrs. Zimmer. "Okay."

Coach and I squeezed out of line and casually strolled

to the Jayhawk bench. We stopped. Coach ran his hand over the smooth white cushion of one of the folding chairs.

He glanced at me out of the corner of his eye and raised his eyebrow. I nodded.

And we turned around and sat. Sat square down on those cushy Jayhawk folding chairs. And then, almost like we'd planned it, we both leaned forward, elbows on our knees, and studied the court, like we were watching a game. A close game, a real nail-biter, down to the buzzer. We were tense. Alert. Ready to go in as soon as the coach called our names.

And for that one bright moment, we were Jayhawks. Iron Man Mike Armstrong and me: mighty, unstoppable Jayhawks. I glanced over at Coach. His face was tense with excitement. His eyes gleamed under the dazzling field-house lights.

Fans on the other side of the court started clapping.

Coach and I looked up, startled.

Applause rippled through the crowd until the whole gym erupted in cheers, every fan staring at the guy in the gray suit who'd just strolled onto the court.

I stared, too. At the guy who towered above everyone around him. At the guy who'd led Stuckey to the state championship three years running and was still doing us proud, breaking NBA records in Phoenix, Arizona. At the guy I'd been staring at—in pictures, anyway—since I was old enough to focus my eyes.

"It's him." The envelope quivered in my hands. "It's really him."

Coach nodded. "Yep." He blew out a big breath. "It is."

He ambled off toward the wooden steps. The real Jayhawk had entered the building.

Thirty-five

Folks still talk about the last shot of the high school state championship game Brett McGrew's senior year. They say McNet was like a freight train that night, driving and scoring and scoring some more. They say the ball had radar. Every time McNet put it up, no matter where he was on the floor, no matter how many guys were in his face, the ball found the hoop and dropped through. They say that's the night he could've broken the record for most points scored in a Kansas high school state championship game. The night he *should've* broken it.

His teammates had gone cold that night. Stone dead cold. They couldn't make a bucket if they'd been standing on a ladder next to the hoop. With six seconds left in regulation, Stuckey was down by one, and McNet needed two points to break the record. Stuckey had the ball, the last shot, and the other team knew who'd take it: Brett McGrew. They double-teamed, triple-teamed, stuck to him like Velcro.

And he probably still could've made the basket. He probably could've muscled past those defenders and put it up. He probably could've sunk the bucket, won the game, and broken the record, all with one stroke of his wrist.

But he saw a teammate cutting toward the basket. A

teammate with a clean, open look.

A teammate who hadn't scored all night.

Nobody in the crowd, nobody in the press, nobody on the bench had any confidence this guy could put it in. The guy's own mother didn't think he could do it. But Brett McGrew did. He knew an open layup was Stuckey's best bet to win the game, so he dished out a perfect pass . . . and his teammate laid it in.

Stuckey won the state championship.

And Brett McGrew gave up his last chance of scoring the most points in a state championship game.

Sports reporters across the state called it the most unselfish move they'd seen in all of basketball.

The afternoon coffee drinkers called it a rotten shame.

Grandma called it proof Brett McGrew had been raised up right. I hoped Grandma knew what she was talking about.

Coach and I took our seats with the rest of the guys, one row behind the seat reserved for Brett McGrew. I watched McNet inch his way across the court. Reporters clustered around him, shoving microphones in his face. Photographers clicked his picture. TV crews filmed his every step. Fans clamored for autographs.

I balanced the brown envelope across my bone-rigid knees and waited. Bragger and I had talked about when I should make my move. About the exact timing. Bragger said I should do it at the first opportunity, the very first minute I met McNet, because I might not get another chance.

And he had a point, but I'd been dreaming of this moment for thirteen years, and I wanted it to be perfect. I really did want that shaft of light to beam down and bathe us in a golden glow. I wanted orchestra music to swell up till it about swallowed us.

I didn't want to finally meet my father while wedged into a third-row seat between Bragger and Coach.

But now that I was actually here, I had to agree with Bragger. I'd do it the first minute I could, no matter where I was sitting. I hadn't been breathing right since we'd gotten on the bus that morning, and I was certain I'd pass out if I waited any longer.

McNet finally made it to our side of the gym. He peeled away from the pack of reporters and glanced up. At me. Right at me. His face broke into a grin, and he bounded up the steps. And I think I did pass out for a second. I know I stopped breathing.

"Hey!" he called out.

Hey? How was I supposed to answer "Hey"? I'd been dreaming of this moment my whole life, and never, not once, had I imagined Brett McGrew saying, "Hey."

"Hey!" he called again. "Mike!"

Mike? I glanced at the guy sitting next to me. At Iron Man Mike Armstrong.

McNet vaulted up the last two steps and grabbed Coach's hand. About shook his arm off. Shook it so hard he pulled Coach clean to his feet. They clapped each other on the back, then Brett McGrew took a step back and looked Coach up and down. Well, mostly down. You think six foot nine looks big on TV, try standing next to it in real life. McNet had a good nine inches on Coach.

"Man, it's been a long time," he said.

And I think Coach said, "Too long." Something like that. It didn't matter. All that mattered was that my father was here. Finally. Standing three feet away.

Coach and Brett McGrew slapped each other on the back again, then McNet turned to the row of thirteen-year-olds who, under strict orders from Coach not to mob the basketball star, were clinging to the edge of their seats, trying to get a better look.

"This must be your team," said McNet.

"Yep. These are my boys." Coach's chest puffed up. He looked, well, proud. Of us. He glanced down the row. "And they're going to explode if I don't introduce you." He rested his hand on my head. "This is our team captain, Kirby Nickel. Without him, I doubt we'd even be here." He glanced at me. "Stand up, Nickel."

I gripped my envelope and stood up. Stood up to meet Brett McGrew. My nose came level with his belt buckle.

McNet held out his hand, and somehow I managed to shake it.

"Team captain," he said. "Pretty big responsibility. You know, I was the captain of our seventh-grade team."

"Uh-huh," I said.

"We won the league championship that year, too, just like your team, so you and I have a lot in common."

"Uh-huh," I said. Smooth, Kirby. Very smooth.

Bragger kneed me in the butt. "Don't talk," he muttered. "It's not your strong suit. Just show him the evidence."

The evidence. Right.

I uncurled my fingers from the envelope. "I—I brought something." I stuck my hand inside and fumbled around. "Something you'll probably, I mean, not probably, but you might, well, maybe, something you maybe might want to see."

I slid my hand from the envelope and held up two photos: the old newspaper picture of Brett McGrew that I'd found in Coach's trash, and the picture Bragger had taken of me lying on my bedroom floor in the same position.

"Hey." Brett McGrew took the newspaper photo from my hand. "I remember this."

I stared at him. "You do?"

"Sure. Hard to forget a big pink heart on somebody's, uh, bottom. Especially when it lands on the front page of the paper." He shook his head at Coach and laughed. "Remember this?"

Coach frowned, cut a sharp look at me, and took the picture from McNet.

Brett McGrew glanced down at the other photo, the one of me lying on the floor with my shorts hiked up. He took it from me. Studied it for a long moment.

He looked at Coach "You didn't tell me about this."

"Tell you about what?" Coach took that photo, too.

"He couldn't," I said. "He didn't know. I didn't think it'd be right to, you know, tell anybody else before I told you. So nobody knew. Except me."

"And me." Bragger squeezed in beside me and held out his hand. "I'm Kirby's cousin, Brandon Barnes. But you can call me Bragger. Welcome to the family."

Brett McGrew shook Bragger's hand and frowned. He looked at Coach, obviously confused. "Family?"

Coach didn't say anything. He was still staring at the picture.

"Kirby, what are you doing to poor Brett?"

I looked up. Grandma. She'd squeezed her way past Mrs. Zimmer and the team and was now hovering behind me.

A smile spread over Brett McGrew's face. "Mrs. Nickel, right?" He reached out to shake Grandma's hand. "Melissa's mom. Wow. I didn't expect to see you here."

"I imagine not," said Grandma. She gripped McNet's hand in both of hers. "How've you been? How's your folks?"

"Great." McNet nodded. "Warm weather agrees with them."

Grandma patted his hand. "I'm glad to hear it. You give them my best next time you see them."

"I sure will."

Okay, this wasn't going the way I'd planned. Not the way I'd planned at all.

"Look," I said. "I've got other stuff." I dug in the

envelope for the number 5 jersey, the one I'd found wrapped around my baby book. I held it up so McNet could see. "Your jersey. From high school. And that's not all." I handed the jersey to Bragger, shoved my hand back into the envelope, and pulled out the medal. "Your league championship medal. Remember this?"

Brett McGrew frowned and peered down at the medal. He didn't say anything.

But Coach did. "Where did you get that?" His voice was soft, almost a whisper. He touched the medal. "I didn't think I'd ever see it again."

Thirty-six

"**Y**ou?" I looked from Coach to Brett McGrew. And back again. Coach was still staring at the medal. "But—"

"We found it in Grandma's prairie dog," said Bragger.

"But—," I said again.

"Prairie dog?" said Brett McGrew.

"Prairie dog." Coach closed his eyes.

"Prairie dog!" Grandma thunked herself in the forehead. "We looked everywhere but the prairie dog."

I stared at Grandma. Then at Coach. "So the medal's . . . ?"

"Mine," he said.

Bragger poked me with his elbow. "See? I told you it might not be McNet's."

"Okay." I grabbed the jersey from Bragger and shook it so Brett McGrew could see the number 5 shimmering under the lights. "But the jersey's yours. And this" —I snatched the old newspaper photo from Coach—"this is you."

Brett McGrew gave me a sad smile. "No," he said. "It's not."

"But . . ." I looked at the picture.

The player in the picture was sliding across the floor on his belly. And you couldn't see his face, not even from the side. He was reaching for the ball, and his outstretched arms blocked his face from the camera's view. The only clear thing in the yellowed old photo was the big number 5 on the player's back.

"But . . ." I looked up. First at Brett McGrew.

Then at Coach.

He nodded. "It's me."

He stared at the photo in my hand. Stared at it like he was trying to stare himself back in time.

"My freshman year," he said. "McNet was still in middle school. Already on his way to basketball stardom. That much was obvious. When he came up to the high school the next year, our coach wanted him to keep the same number he wore all through middle school. Number five. Thought a new number might jinx him. You know how basketball folks get." He raised an eyebrow. "Some teams are so superstitious they change into their underwear at halftime. So McNet kept number five, and I switched to number twenty-three. Kept my old number five jersey, though. Would've been too small for McNet." He touched the shimmering number 5. "Your mother promised she'd keep it safe. She always did keep her promises."

Coach stopped talking then. He rubbed a hand across his mouth. And finally looked at me. Looked at me and looked at me and looked at me, for thirteen years, it seemed. A smile threatened to break out at the corners of his mouth, and this time he didn't stop it. He let it slide right out there onto his face.

He raised an eyebrow at me.

I nodded.

And then, almost like we'd planned it, we hiked up the bottoms of our matching Jayhawk boxers. And there, on the backs of our legs, were matching pink hearts.

And I know this part sounds crazy, like something I made up, but at that moment, a shaft of light really did beam down, and music really did swell up around us. Okay, so the light was the blinding bulb of a TV camera aimed right at our butts, and the music was the KU pep band blasting out the KU fight song to get the crowd riled up before the game.

Still, somehow it was perfect. Somehow it was the way I'd always imagined it.

I looked at Coach. My father.

I'd finally found my father.

Thirty-seven

"**W**ell." Grandma took a good, hard look at Coach's pink heart. "If I'd known about that, it would've answered a lot of questions, wouldn't it?" She peered up at Coach through her bifocals. "I always thought you were a good boy." She gave Coach's face a good, hard look, too. "You were good for my Melissa. You better be good for my Kirby, too."

She gave Coach's hand a squeeze, then left Coach and me to ourselves. She said it was because we needed time alone to sort things out. I think secretly she just didn't want to miss tip-off.

Coach—my father—and I spent the first half of the game talking. Yeah, me and Coach. The kid whose tongue gets wrapped around his tonsils every time he speaks, and the guy whose main form of communication is a grunt. We didn't look at each other much. Just sat there, side by side, watching the game, eating nachos, and figuring things out. Things we'd both been wondering about.

Like, for instance, why my mom never told anybody who my father was. Turns out she *had* been protecting him, just like I thought. Just like I told Bragger. Only, instead of protecting Brett McGrew while he fielded offers from every big-time basketball program in the country, she was protecting Mike Armstrong, who'd managed to land a scholarship to Kaw Valley Community College and was scrapping and scraping to make a name for himself in junior college ball so maybe a big-time program would recruit him as a transfer.

"I thought it could happen." Coach shook his head. "I really thought it could. You know why? Because of your mother. Because she thought I could do anything. Everybody else noticed Brett McGrew. But your mom, she noticed me. I wouldn't have gotten half as far if it weren't for her telling me I could."

And she kept telling him that, too, till one day, when he was off at college, eating, sleeping, breathing basketball, she called him. Said she couldn't see him anymore. Said she'd found someone else. She didn't tell him that someone else was me.

"And I believed it." Coach ran a hand across his mouth. "Why wouldn't I? She always deserved better than me, anyway. I figured I was lucky it took her as long as it did to catch on."

I sat there for a long time after that, chewing my nachos. "I wish I'd known her," I said finally.

"Yeah." Coach stared straight ahead at the basketball court. "I wish you had, too."

Just before halftime, somebody from the athletic department came and got us. We stripped down to our silky Jayhawk boxers and lined up at the end of the court, waiting for the half to end so the University of Kansas could retire Brett McGrew's jersey.

Camera bulbs flashed. The Jayhawks and their opponents thundered up and down the court. Glittery cheerleaders bounced and yelled and shook their pom-poms. I stood at the edge of it, in my underwear, waiting to play basketball with my father on national television.

"So." Bragger squeezed in between me and Coach. "What should I call you, now that we're family? Mike? Uncle Mike? Uncle Iron Man?"

Coach shot him a dark look.

"Okay, maybe not." Bragger nodded. "Maybe we'll just leave it at Coach for now. Or no, I got it—Uncle Coach."

Coach closed his eyes and shook his head.

The buzzer honked. Halftime. The Kansas Jayhawks jogged off the court. The Stuckey seventh-grade Prairie Dogs jogged on. A guy from the athletic department strolled out to center court with a microphone and a framed Brett McGrew number 5 jersey. He gave a little speech, telling all about McNet's astonishing college basketball career. Then Brett McGrew took the microphone and gave his own little speech, thanking KU, the fans, his college coach, his parents.

"But my career wouldn't have been possible without all the folks back home in Stuckey who believed in me," he said.

He waved a hand toward Mrs. Zimmer and Mr. Dobbs, who had risen to their feet. Mrs. Zimmer fanned herself with one hand while holding her chest with the other. I thought she was going to faint dead away, right there in the third row. Mr. Dobbs had traded his John Deere cap for a Jayhawk basketball cap, and now he pulled it off his head and held it over his heart.

"I'd also like to thank a fellow player from those Stuckey years," said Brett McGrew. "A guy who, even then, was helping his teammates, including me, play better basketball. The Stuckey seventh-grade coach, Mike Armstrong, who led his team to a perfect fourteen and O record this year."

The crowd clapped. Coach's face went red. He studied the toes of his shoes. Mrs. Zimmer beamed. Brett McGrew had announced our record on national television, and it was a better record than she ever could have imagined.

Brett McGrew handed the microphone back, and we started our scrimmage. Four players and Coach on one team, four players and McNet on the other, two subs for each. I was on Coach's team. He'd picked me. First. I almost didn't know what to do. I'd never been picked first choosing up sides before.

We tipped off, and the two teams rumbled up and down the floor, trading baskets. About halfway through the scrimmage, I picked off a pass. I fired the ball to Coach, and he thundered up the court for an easy layup.

Easy if he'd been playing with mere mortals. But we had a future hall-of-famer on the court. Brett McGrew whipped past Coach and set up in front of the hoop.

Coach didn't stop. Didn't slow down. He barreled toward McNet. Right toward him. He went in for the layup, but instead of going straight up, instead of charging into McNet and committing the offensive foul, he pushed off and spun around to the other side of the basket.

Th-bumpf.

The ball hit the backboard and swished through the net.

Iron Man Mike Armstrong's spinning layup. Executed perfectly.

The crowd cheered. Or, at least, the part of the crowd that hadn't wandered off to buy Coke and nachos. Coach's team cheered, too. Brett McGrew slapped Coach a high five.

But Coach didn't look at them. Not at the crowd or the other guys or even Brett McGrew. As the ball dropped through the hoop, Coach turned and looked down the court, searching, till his gaze landed on me. He nodded, smiled, and pointed, the way a shooter does to thank the guy who fed him the ball.

I nodded, smiled, and pointed back.

And then I just stood there. The other guys whooped past me down the court. But for a second, I stood there, in the shadow of the banners and the scoreboard and all that history. Stood there and took it all in.

Because sometimes the things you want aren't possible.

Sometimes they're not even good for you.

But sometimes, even if you kick the ball out of bounds when you dribble, even if your jump shots look like bounce passes, even if you end up on national television wearing nothing but your underpants—

Coach backpedaled past me, and as he did, he reached out and ruffled my hair.

—sometimes the thing you want most in the world really does want you back.

ABOUT THE AUTHOR

L. D. Harkrader never played underwear basketball but did have a recurring nightmare about walking into the school cafeteria wearing nothing but pajamas. "I'm sure the dream meant I was afraid people would see who I really was," says L. D. "In telling Kirby's story, I hope I show readers they shouldn't be afraid to let people see who they are. Who they are is okay."

Like Kirby, L. D. grew up in a small town in Kansas and is a rabid Jayhawks basketball fan. *Airball: My Life in Briefs* is L. D. Harkrader's first fiction.